'Twas just before Christmas, and all over Elk Creek
Tongues were a-flappin' with the news of the week
A princess was visiting, with staff and a child,
And seeking a rancher. Wasn't that wild?

Now Belle (that's the princess) had a story to tell
And she wasn't certain it all would end well
She had to be sure that her friend's child, a boy
Would be raised by his father with love and
   with joy.

So Belle and her bodyguard, companion and babe
Moved in with the ranchers, the Misters McCade
And as Montana, and Christmas, and love worked
   their charms
Guess who fell passionately into whose arms?

Dear Reader,

It is the season of giving. And Arabella Bravo-Calabretti, Princess of Montedoro, has come to the small Montana town of Elk Creek bearing a gift beyond price. He's eighteen months old and his name is Benjamin.

Horse rancher Preston McCade has a good life, a solid, stable, productive life. It's a life he's just fine with, though deep in his heart he has that nagging feeling that the most important things have passed him by. Once, he planned on marriage and a family. It didn't work out. He hasn't tried again.

But then he meets Princess Arabella and soon enough, the child named Ben. And all of a sudden, Christmas is more than just a day in December. Preston's life is full of promise again and more than one miracle is within his grasp. He just needs to be brave enough to reach out and claim the love that's waiting for him.

Happy holidays, everyone! May this blessed season bring you the most important gifts—the ones of love and family.

Yours always,

Christine

THE RANCHER'S CHRISTMAS PRINCESS

CHRISTINE RIMMER

Recycling programs
for this product may
not exist in your area.

ISBN-13: 978-0-373-65711-7

THE RANCHER'S CHRISTMAS PRINCESS

Books by Christine Rimmer

CHRISTINE RIMMER

came to her profession the long way around. Before settling down to write about the magic of romance, she'd been everything from an actress to a salesclerk to a waitress. Now that she's finally found work that suits her perfectly, she insists she never had a problem keeping a job—she was merely gaining "life experience" for her future as a novelist. Christine is grateful not only for the joy she finds in writing, but for what waits when the day's work is through: a man she loves who loves her right back, and the privilege of watching their children grow and change day to day. She lives with her family in Oregon. Visit Christine at www.christinerimmer.com.

For MSR
Always

Chapter One

News traveled fast in Elk Creek, Montana.

And the presence of a real, live princess in town? That definitely qualified as news.

Her Highness's name was Arabella. Arabella Bravo-Calabretti. And her mother ruled some tiny, rich country in the Mediterranean Sea. Princess Arabella had taken three side-by-side rooms at the Drop On Inn on Main Street. Word was she had a baby in tow. She'd also brought along a big-eyed middle-aged lady and a bodyguard as well.

In Elk Creek, where things tended to get pretty quiet during the long, snowy winter, visiting royalty was big news indeed.

As a rule, horse rancher Preston McCade would have given no thought and less attention to any princess, in Elk Creek or otherwise. However, Her Highness Arabella had been asking questions—about him. She'd arrived in town on a Sunday in early December. Preston got a call that very evening informing him that the princess wanted to get in touch with him.

And on Monday morning bright and early, when he stopped in at Colson's Feed and Seed to check on an order, Betsy Colson beamed him the biggest smile he'd seen on her freckled face in all the years he'd known her.

"Pres." Betsy slid out from behind the counter. "You heard there's a princess in town?"

"Good morning to you, too, Betsy."

"I heard it from Dee Everhart who got it straight from RaeNell." RaeNell and Larry Seabuck owned and managed the Drop On Inn. "She's from Montedoro, this princess. You ever heard of Montedoro? It's on the coast of France. They say it's beautiful there. Palm trees. Casinos. Balmy beaches, the sun shining practically year-round."

Pres removed his hat and tapped it against his thigh to knock off the snow. "Speaking of weather, it's supposed to snow on and off all day. Tomorrow, too."

Betsy, who'd been trying to push him around since way back when she was two years ahead of him at Elk Creek Elementary, braced her fists on her narrow hips. "Did you *hear* what I just told you?"

"I heard yesterday. RaeNell called me out at the ranch to tell me some princess was looking for me."

Betsy widened her eyes—and lowered her voice. "Dee said that RaeNell says that the princess wants to *speak* with you, Pres."

"Well, then I'm sure she'll be calling me. I told RaeNell to give her my number."

Betsy's pale brows drew together over her pointy nose. "What do you think a princess wants with *you?*"

"Not a clue. Any news on those supplements I ordered?"

"They'll be in by Wednesday, guaranteed."

"All right, then." He turned for the door.

Betsy called after him. "She's staying at the Drop On Inn, you know. You could just stop in there, find out what she's after...."

"See you Wednesday, Betsy." He put his hat back on and pulled open the door. Ducking under the mistletoe tacked to the door frame, he got out of there before Betsy could tell him more things he *could* be doing.

The snow had let up. And the Drop On Inn was down at the end of Main Street. He went ahead and walked over there before stopping in at Safeway to pick up a few groceries. He *was* kind of curious. Might as well find out what business this princess thought she had with him.

Larry Seabuck, slim and stooped with thinning gray hair, stood behind the check-in desk when Pres entered the motel's pine-paneled lobby. "Preston, how's the world treating you?"

"Can't complain. I heard you had a visitor who's looking for me."

"The princess." Larry said it reverently and just a tad possessively, too.

"What room is she in?" Pres took off his hat again.

Larry frowned. "RaeNell said she called you—and when you said it was all right, she gave Her Highness your phone number."

"Could you buzz the lady's room? Tell her I'm here and willing to talk to her."

"Ahem. Well. She isn't in just now."

Pres rested an elbow on the check-in counter, which had fake Christmas garland tacked in loops all around the rim and a small tree decked with blinking lights down at the far end. "You're looking a little squirrelly, Larry. Why don't you just say what's on your mind?"

Larry's wire-rimmed glasses had slid down his nose. He eased them back up. "Well, a woman of quality. An aristocrat. And she's our guest. We've had two calls from reporters, asking if she's staying here. She's asked us to say she has no comment and doesn't wish to be disturbed. We want to respect her privacy."

Pres, who in recent years hadn't found a whole lot to laugh about in life, suddenly realized he was suppressing a chuckle. "She good lookin', this princess?"

"Uh. Well. Very attractive. Of course. Ahem. Yes."

"Larry, I believe you are smitten. You better watch out. Someone will tell RaeNell."

"Oh, now, Preston. It's nothing like that." Larry blinked several times in succession. "No, not at all."

"Just tell me where I can find her. I promise to be on my best behavior."

Larry pressed his thin lips together. "You don't even know how to talk to a princess."

"Suppose you clue me in, Larry?"

"Ahem. Don't sit in her presence unless she invites you to. Call her 'Your Highness' the first time you address her. After that, call her 'ma'am.'"

"She told you all this?"

Larry sniffed. "Of course not. I looked it up. On Wikipedia."

"Well, all right. So where do I find her?"

Larry gave in at last. "Oh, have it your way. Breakfast. She's at breakfast." He threw out a pale, skinny hand in the general direction of the Sweet Stop Diner across the street.

"Thanks, Larry. You have a fine day."

Belle saw him coming. He was tall and ruggedly handsome. He marched right up to the booth where she sat alone, removed his cowboy hat and addressed her politely. "Your Highness, I'm Preston McCade. I heard you've been looking for me."

Her bodyguard, Marcus, who stood near the diner's front door, watched her for a sign that he should intervene. Belle met Marcus's waiting eyes and gave a quick shake of her head. Then she granted the large rancher a cool, pleasant smile. "Yes, I have been hoping to meet you, Mr. McCade." She indicated the empty seat across from her. "Please, join me."

Everyone in the diner was watching them. Belle could *feel* their breath-held regard. It was so quiet that a person could have heard a feather whisper its way to the floor as the rancher shrugged out of his sheepskin jacket and hung it up on the hook beside the booth along with his hat. Beneath the jacket, he wore a plain cotton shirt that was the same pale, cool blue as his eyes. His jeans were worn and his rawhide Western boots looked lived-in.

Blue eyes, she thought. *A lovely light blue just like Ben's....*

"The usual, Pres?" the waitress called out from over behind the long counter.

"Sounds good, Selma." He slid into the booth.

The waitress stuck an order on the metal wheel in the window to the kitchen. Then she picked up a coffeepot and sauntered over to the booth. Preston McCade turned his mug up and she filled it. She topped off Belle's cup, too.

The rancher sipped and set down the mug. By then the waitress had left them. "Planning on being in town long, ma'am?"

"Please." She spoke softly. "Call me Belle. My visit here is…open-ended."

They regarded each other. His gaze was level and steady. He had strong, broad shoulders and a square jaw with a nice, manly cleft in it. She could see how Anne might have found him attractive. Any woman would.

And not only was he attractive, but there was also some-

thing steady about him. Something thoughtful and dignified and reserved. Her instinctive response was that he
would be someone a person could depend on. She felt that
it wouldn't be difficult at all to come to like him, to respect
him. She was glad for that. She'd been worried about what
she would do if she *didn't* like him.

She'd been worried about a lot of things. She was still
worried, if the truth were known, just tied up in knots over
this whole situation.

And her heart ached. For her lost friend. For sweet little Ben…

Oh, dear Lord. How could she do this? How could Anne
have asked this of her? She shouldn't *have* to do this….

"You okay, ma'am—I mean, Belle?" McCade spoke low,
with what really did sound like honest concern. He was
leaning toward her a little.

Suddenly, she couldn't bear to meet his eyes. She looked
down at his hands bracketing the heavy coffee mug. They
were strong hands, big hands. Capable. Calloused. Hard-
working hands.

Was his life…difficult? Harsh? How harsh?

So very many things she needed to know. Too many,
really. Obligation dragged on her like chains.

She composed her expression and then made herself
raise her head again: "Yes, I'm all right. Thank you." She
glanced out the window. "It's snowing again."

He nodded. "You'd best not make your visit *too* open-
ended. Stick around another week or so, you won't be getting out of Montana until the spring thaw."

"I think I shall have to take my chances as far as the
weather goes, Mr. McCade."

"Preston."

She felt a smile blooming. Almost. "Preston."

He nodded at her nearly full plate. "Eat. Your food will get cold."

She wasn't hungry. Not anymore. At the sight of him striding so purposefully toward her, her appetite had fled. Still, she picked up her fork again.

Pres sipped his coffee and tried not to stare at the princess across from him.

She was good-looking, all right. With all that shiny brown hair and those fine, almond-shaped whiskey-colored eyes. Her skin had a glow to it. He bet it was soft as velvet to a man's touch. And she was classy, too. Polite. Soft-voiced. No wonder Larry had a crush on her.

His food came—a thick steak, four eggs, home fries, toast and a generous slice of hot apple pie on the side. He tucked into the meal, thinking that he liked the direct, no-nonsense way she'd met his gaze. She seemed kind of serious, though. Kind of sad. Like something was weighing on her mind.

Then again, he was pretty damn serious himself as a rule. After all, life was tough. Then you died.

"Have you lived here in Montana all your life, Preston?"

"Except for four years of college in Utah. I live at the family ranch. The McCade Ranch. It's a ways out of town. We breed and train horses. Quarter horses, mostly, for ranch work."

"The quarter horse. That most American of breeds. Great sprinters. So agile. Perfectly suited to work on a ranch."

His opinion of her went up another notch. "You know horses."

"My father was raised on a ranch," she said. "In Texas. Near San Antonio. I have a cousin, Luke, who lives on that ranch now. Luke raises quarter horses, too, as a matter of fact."

"Your father's American, then?"

"He took Montedoran citizenship when he married my mother. But yes, he was born here in America. I've ridden since I was small. We all have, my brothers and sisters and me. My sister Alice is the true horsewoman of the family, though. Do you raise cattle also?"

"We do run cattle, yes. A small herd. But we're mostly a horse operation. I'm in partnership with my dad and the ranch has been in the family for four generations. I'm pretty proud of our breeding program. Our horses are steady-natured, good for ranch work. They also perform well in rodeos across a range of events. We have two fine thoroughbreds standing at stud." Whoa. He'd said a mouthful. As a rule, he wasn't a man to fall all over himself bragging about his operation. He concentrated on his food again.

She asked, "Any brothers or sisters?"

"Just me and the old man."

She leaned in a little. "You smiled. Because of your father?"

He shrugged. "You'd have to meet him. My father considers himself a charmer."

"But he's not?"

"I generally let people make up their own minds about that. But be warned. He'll talk your ear off if you give him half a chance."

"And your mother?"

"She passed on."

"I'm sorry."

He shrugged. "It was a long time ago. I was only a kid."

"That must have been hard. For you. And your father."

"Like I said, a long time ago." He had a few questions of his own. One in particular: What was it she needed to see him about? But she seemed to want to…get to know him a little, for some reason. And he realized that was just fine with him. He was curious about her, too. "How about *your* family?"

She sipped her coffee. "Both of my parents are still living and in good health."

"You said you had sisters and you mentioned brothers, too?"

"I have four sisters and four brothers."

"That's quite a royal family."

"Montedoro is a principality," she explained. "That means we, the ruling family, are not, strictly speaking, considered royal."

"So your father's not a king?"

"Actually, it's my mother who rules Montedoro."

Right. RaeNell had told him that, now that he thought about it. "You said your dad was born an American…"

She nodded. "They met in Los Angeles. My father used to be an actor. He did well for himself, even won an Oscar for best actor in a supporting role."

"But he gave all that up when he met your mother?"

"Yes, he did. When my mother took the throne he became His Serene Highness Evan, Prince Consort of Montedoro—and no, my mother is not a queen. She's the sovereign princess."

"I see," he said. Though he didn't, not really. He only thought that her world and his were galaxies apart.

Which had him feeling suddenly awkward and foolish. He'd been talking way too much, acting like a rube, a hayseed way too full of himself, all puffed up to be having breakfast with this amber-eyed beauty from a long, long ways out of town.

Come on now. Exactly what business did she have with him? Whatever it was, she sure wasn't in any rush to get down to it. He pushed his plate away, wiped his mouth and set his napkin on the table.

The princess could take a hint. "I wonder if we might speak in private…" she cautiously suggested. He couldn't say he blamed her for wanting to take the conversation elsewhere. The low murmur of other voices filled the diner now. But he had no doubt that every ear in the place remained cocked toward their booth.

He thought again about how he had nothing in common with her, how she was out of his league and way out of his reach. How he was only here to find out why she was asking around about him. He reminded himself how he had no interest in women anyway, not since his fiancée dumped him for that jackass Monty Polk over two years ago now.

Plus, RaeNell had mentioned a baby, hadn't she? That the princess had a baby with her. She wore no wedding ring. But why would she bring a baby to Elk Creek unless it belonged to her?

He went ahead and asked her. "Belle, are you married?"

She answered without hesitation. "No, Preston, I'm not."

Then what about the baby?

But he couldn't quite get those words out. He'd been raised to mind his manners around a lady. And he didn't know her well enough to ask her something as personal as that.

Instead, he shocked the hell out of himself by asking, "Would you have dinner with me?"

Chapter Two

The princess had agreed that he would pick her up at the Drop On Inn at seven. Pres was there right on time, freshly showered and shaved, wearing tan slacks and a sport jacket under his winter coat—and feeling like something way too close to a damn fool.

RaeNell was behind the desk, hanging miniature red balls on the little Christmas tree. "Lookin' pretty spiffy there, Pres. I'll tell her you're here."

He gave her a nod of acknowledgment and wondered how RaeNell knew that he was there to pick up Belle. Then he decided not to stew over it. RaeNell *always* knew way more than she had any business knowing.

She picked up the phone and pushed a button. "Hello, Lady Charlotte. Please tell Her Highness that Preston Mc-Cade is waiting in the lobby....Yes. Thank you." RaeNell put the phone down. "She'll be right down."

"Great."

RaeNell stood back to admire the little tree, then stepped close again to move an ornament to a spot nearer the top. "Where are you taking her? The Bull's Eye? Of course you are. Where else you gonna get a decent steak in this town?"

Pres said nothing. He didn't need to. RaeNell had always been perfectly capable of carrying on a conversation all by herself.

RaeNell folded her arms and braced them on the counter and pitched her voice to a whisper that somehow managed to ring out clear as a shout. "So what did she want from you? What's it all about? Come on, you can tell me. You know I will never tell a living soul."

"I don't know what she wants from me, RaeNell. She hasn't said yet."

"But everyone *saw* you having breakfast with her, the two of you yakking away like you're the best of friends."

He only looked at her. He kept his expression untroubled, although he was at least as curious as RaeNell as to what it might be that Belle wanted from him. "Sorry, she didn't say."

The concrete stairs to the upper floor were visible through the window that gave a view of the parking lot. He watched Belle and her bodyguard descend.

RaeNell pasted on a big smile and stopped leaning on the counter. The bodyguard opened the door and Belle sailed through wearing a long wool coat. Beneath the hem of the coat he saw she wore black boots with low heels. At breakfast, she'd worn a cashmere sweater and tan pants, with tan boots to match. He liked the way she dressed. Simply and practically. Expensive, but not flashy.

She met his eyes. "Preston, hello." The dark, cold Montana night suddenly seemed cozy, bright as a new day.

He offered his arm. She stepped up and took it. He felt

like a million bucks—or maybe two million. The body-guard opened the door for them.

As soon as they were outside where RaeNell couldn't eavesdrop, he said, "The restaurant's just down the street. We can walk, if you don't mind a few snow flurries and a little gale-force wind."

She gripped his arm a fraction tighter, moved in just an inch closer. He got a whiff of her perfume. It was like her. Subtle, but so tempting. "I would love to walk."

He asked, "Your bodyguard have a name?"

"Marcus."

"You can leave Marcus behind. I promise not to give you any reason to need backup."

She let out a small, resigned sigh. "Marcus goes where I go. If I dismissed him, he would still follow us. He doesn't take orders from me. His job is to protect me and he's very…committed to his job."

"Even if you don't need protecting?"

"Yes."

"That doesn't make a whole lot of sense."

"Sadly, in this day and age, you just never know. A little over five years ago, my brother Alexander was kidnapped in Afghanistan. He eventually escaped and he's home safe and happily married now, but the kidnapping forced my family to face a few realities. Whenever we travel now, we have security round-the-clock."

He'd read about her brother's kidnapping. That afternoon, he'd spent an hour on the internet learning what he could about Belle and her family. "I'm sorry to hear about your brother."

"He's doing well now. Truly. But Marcus will be accompanying us."

"Fair enough."

She had her face tipped up to him. Her eyes seemed almost golden in the light that spilled out the lobby windows. She clutched his arm a little tighter. "Then shall we go?"

"This way." He touched her gloved hand where it wrapped around his forearm. They started off down the street.

The bodyguard fell back several paces. It wasn't that hard to pretend he wasn't there.

The Bull's Eye Steakhouse and Casino was in a brick storefront between the Upper Crust Bakery and Elk Creek Cleaners. The sign out front was a target with a giant red arrow sticking out of the center. Miniature multicolored Christmas lights framed the front windows and the door.

Inside, nothing had changed since the last time Pres ate there. The walls were paneled in bead board up to the chair rails and decorated with a lot of bad paintings of cowboys on trail drives. The tablecloths? Vinyl, printed with Western scenes. The chairs had red vinyl cushions and backs. There was a full bar. In the back was the "casino," which consisted of two poker tables and a row of gambling machines. From the dining room, faintly, you could hear the never-ending sound effects from the machines.

The Bull's Eye wasn't exactly jumping that early December night. Pres had called ahead and told the owner which table he wanted. It was the one tucked into that quiet corner, across from the bar.

Daisy Littlejohn, the owner's daughter, greeted them, waited for Pres to hang their coats and his hat on the coat tree by the door next to the Christmas tree and then led them to the table he'd asked for. Once they were settled in the red vinyl chairs, she handed them menus. "Wayne will be right with you."

Wayne, the waiter, knew his job. They went through the business of ordering drinks and food. He got all that out of the way quickly. In no time, they were left alone with a bread basket and a nice bottle of red wine.

"It's not fancy," Pres said, "but I think you'll like that rib eye you ordered."

"I'm sure I will." She sipped from her water glass.

Pres had ended up facing the door. The bodyguard stood by the row of chairs in front of the register, out of the way. He seemed to be good at blending in. Daisy was behind the register counter, fiddling with some receipts or something. She seemed totally oblivious to the big, silent fellow standing right there beside her.

"I looked you up on the internet," Pres confessed.

Belle nodded, apparently not in any way surprised. "Did you find out anything interesting?"

He buttered a hunk of bread. "I learned about what happened to your brother."

She nodded. "It was terrible for all of us. We were sure he had died. But he returned to us. And it's over now. His wife, who is like a sister to me, is expecting twins next month. They are very much in love, Lili and Alex."

"I read that your Lili is a princess from the island country of Alagonia."

"Yes. Lili's the crown princess, the heir presumptive."

He chuckled. She amused him to no end with her talk of princes and crowns, of thrones and titles. "And that means?"

"Lili's an only child. If her father, the king, never has a son, she will rule Alagonia one day. She's called the heir presumptive because it's *presumed* that she will one day be queen, barring the birth of a male heir. If she were a man, she would be called the heir *apparent* and her position as first in line of succession would be secure, regardless of any future children her father might have."

He studied her expression. "Somehow, you don't approve of that?"

"Well, I think it's somewhat…backward. As though men were born naturally superior to women, naturally more suited to rule and therefore should take precedence. Everyone in the modern world knows that's completely untrue."

Pres set down his butter knife. "You expecting me to argue that point with you?"

"Were you planning to?"

"Not a chance."

She sent him a sideways look. "Good thinking, Preston."

He moved on to a safer subject. "I also read that you're a nurse, that you work with Nurses Without Boundaries."

"Yes. In my family, we believe in being useful. I don't do a lot of hands-on nursing, but I *am* able to help raise awareness—and necessary funds—to get supplies and medical personnel where they're most needed around the world." She was so damn easy on the eyes. He could have sat there across from her forever, listening to her beautiful voice, watching her face, on the lookout for a hint of a smile. And he really was impressed that she was a nurse. She'd gone and gotten herself an education in a useful profession, even though she probably had money running out her ears and would never actually need to work. "What else did you learn about me?" she asked.

He swallowed a bite of bread. "Your oldest brother, the heir to the throne, is a widower with two children."

She picked up her wine, took a small sip. "What else?"

"Your second-born brother married a lawyer from Texas who happened to be the mother of his son."

She chuckled. A beautiful sound. "That's a long story. For another time."

"None of your sisters are married. Neither is your one

other brother, Alexander's twin, Damien. I also read all about your mother and father and how they met."

She gave an elegant shrug. "How did *your* parents meet?"

"My dad was six, my mom was five. It was her first day of kindergarten."

"Ah," she said. "Love fated from childhood."

"I don't know about that. The story goes that he chased her around the playground. She ran away screaming, tripped and needed seven stitches in her chin. She didn't let him near her for years after that."

"At least it was a memorable meeting."

"It certainly was."

Wayne brought their salads. They ate, talking easily. Of her life. Of his. The steaks came—and were terrific as always. He told her he was an agriculture major in college. She said she'd gotten her nursing degree in America, at Duke University.

He knew that this dinner was supposed to be an opportunity for her to get down to whatever it was that she needed to discuss with him. Didn't matter. It felt like a date to Preston. A real date. A successful date, the kind of date that has a man thinking he will ask this woman out again. The kind of date that makes the world seem new and fresh and full of promise.

He kept reminding himself that it really wasn't a date. That any minute now, she was going to get down to it, to tell him what was going on.

But she didn't tell him. They had coffee and the Bull's Eye's famous bread pudding.

And she remained not the least forthcoming as to why she'd been asking around town about him. He probably should have been more bothered about that, should have pushed at her to get on with it.

But he wasn't all that bothered and he didn't feel like pushing. He was enjoying himself too much. By the time he'd swallowed the last of his bread pudding, he was starting to think he didn't really care if she ever told him why she'd been looking for him.

The bodyguard was still waiting patiently by the door when they went to get their coats. Pres helped Belle into hers.

She looked back over her shoulder at him. "Thank you, Preston."

He had his hands on her slim shoulders. He never wanted to take them away. And he wasn't ready for the evening to end. "How about a drive out to my ranch?"

"Yes, I would like that."

He let go of her reluctantly and reached for his hat. "It's a half-an-hour ride," he warned because it only seemed fair to let her know the trip would take a while. "A half hour each way."

"That's fine. Marcus will follow us and drive me back. That way you won't have to make two trips."

"I don't mind making two trips." The words came out husky and full of meanings he hadn't intended to put in them.

She only said softly, "That's lovely. But Marcus *will* be following us. He might as well bring me back."

Belle was becoming annoyed with herself.

She should have told him by now. The longer she dragged it out, the more upset he was likely to be when she finally got down to it.

But every time she started to edge up on the difficult things that needed saying, she would glance across the table into those sky-blue eyes of his and…her tongue was suddenly a slab of lead in her mouth, inert and unresponsive. Incapable of forming the necessary words.

Because, honestly, how does one tell a man such a thing? How does one deliver such news?

She should have planned better. She should have rehearsed what she might say, practiced how to…lead up to it. Because she wasn't leading up to it and the longer she stalled, the worse it was going to be when she finally delivered the truth.

The drive out to his ranch was a quiet one. He wasn't a man who felt it necessary to fill every silence with words. Even with her nerves on edge from all she had yet to say, she appreciated that about him. He was good with silence. At peace with it.

There were so many things she liked about him. Too many. Her response to him was distressingly positive on more than one level. She found him much too attractive. It made her feel…all turned around somehow.

Maybe she really shouldn't have rushed into this. Her mother and father had urged her to hire a private investigator to check Preston out before she approached him. They'd seen no reason why she had to head straight for Montana after the funeral.

But she'd had other ideas. She'd agreed to hire the investigator, but she'd also decided to come straightaway to meet him. In the end, it was going to have to be her decision anyway. She didn't want to dawdle over it, growing more and more attached to Ben as he grew more attached to her.

Better to get moving on what needed doing, to…get it over with.

She was a good judge of character and so far Preston had done nothing to raise any red flags with her. On the contrary, he seemed to her a solid, trustworthy man. A responsible man. When she'd asked the chatty motel owner about him, the woman had said he was gruff and not an easy man to know, that he'd only gotten more withdrawn after a "disappointment in love" two years before. Belle had wanted to ask the woman for details about that "disappointment."

But she hadn't. It would have felt too much like gossiping. Still, after what Mrs. Seabuck had said about him, she'd worried he would be hard to know.

And then she'd met him and found him much too easy to talk to. He hadn't been gruff or withdrawn in the least, not with her anyway.

She could find no excuse to keep the truth from him. She needed to follow through on her dear friend's final request.

Anne had wanted it this way....

Anne.

Just thinking her name brought a fresh surge of pain. Her friend had been gone for only ten days. Maybe she should have listened to her parents, waited for the investigator's report at least.

All she really wanted was to keep Ben with her, to raise him as her own.

But that wasn't to be. In the end, she was honor bound to carry through and do what Anne requested.

How to get started, though? How to get the all-important words out of her mouth?

Dear Lord, she still didn't know.

It was snowing lightly, the white flakes flying at the windshield out of the darkness. So beautiful. So cold.

The land was bare and rolling with a silvery glow about it. Staggered, leaning fences lined the slopes to either side of the two-lane highway. Farther out, she could see the dark shapes of evergreens. The sky was endless—cloudy overhead, but clear far in the distance. On the crests of the mountain ridges way ahead, beneath the lowering dark clouds, she could see a band of cobalt studded with stars.

"Here we are," Preston said. Neither of them had spoken for several minutes. He turned the four-door pickup truck onto a smaller road. The lights of Marcus's SUV beamed in through the rear window as the bodyguard swung in behind them.

Thick evergreens, several rows of them on either side, lined the curving road. "Ponderosa pines," he said. "They make a good windbreak."

The snow had stopped. They rode between the thick stands of dark trees. And then the road opened up. There was a rustic arched gate with a sign: McCade Ranch. Beyond the gate, she saw barns and sheds, pastures and corrals, the land rolling in the distance. Farther out, those craggy peaks poked into the sky.

There were two houses facing off across a wide yard and circular driveway from each other. They were both two-story, of wood and natural stone, the smaller house seeming almost a miniature of the larger one. There were lights on in both houses. Nearer the barn, she saw another house, more rustic, like a cabin. There were lights on inside that one, too.

Preston parked in front of the largest house. Marcus pulled in behind him and was at her door, opening it for her, before Preston could get there.

She got out and went to meet Preston as he came around the front of the pickup. "Marcus will need to go in first, if that's all right? To…have a look around."

Preston shrugged. "Whatever it takes." He turned to the bodyguard. "Go ahead. It's not locked." Marcus went up the steps and disappeared inside. Preston offered his arm and she took it. They proceeded up the steps at a slower pace. "So…do we wait out here until he gives the okay?"

She felt her cheeks redden. Really, all these security protocols did become tiresome. "It should be only a minute or two. And the good news is, once he gives the all clear, if you ever invite me back, he won't insist on doing this again."

"You sure?" Blue eyes teased.

"I promise." Her gaze drifted to his mouth. It was a fine mouth, firm and yet well-shaped. She wondered what it might feel like pressed to hers—which was a completely unacceptable and inappropriate thing to be wondering.

She was not going to kiss this man. She hardly *knew* this man. This evening was *not* about kisses and she desperately needed to remember that.

"Don't look now, but here comes my father." Preston's gaze had shifted. He was looking out across the front yard. Which meant maybe he hadn't seen her staring at his lips—she hoped. "Whatever he says, don't believe a word of it."

She turned to look. A tall, rangy white-haired man with a thick, walrus-worthy moustache came striding toward them dressed in a pair of jeans that had seen better days and one of those waffle-weave shirts that looked like it doubled as his pajamas. He had bushy gray brows and a definite gleam in his eyes.

"Preston," he said, his voice deep and rumbling and full of good humor. "Where's your manners? You bring a lady home, you know I need to meet her. It's only right I give her warning about you." The old guy's mustache twitched. He gave Belle a wink. "I'm Silas. The charming half of the family." He offered a leathery hand.

Belle took it. "Arabella. Please call me Belle."

He enclosed her hand between both of his. His gray eyes twinkled down at her. "I heard about you. They say you're a princess…."

"Back it down a notch, Dad," Preston muttered dryly.

The door opened and Marcus emerged. "All clear, ma'am."

Silas patted her hand before letting it go. "A bodyguard. I can tell by that thing in his ear. And the lack of any facial expression whatsoever."

Preston appeared to be suppressing a groan. "Why don't we go in?" He gestured at the open door.

"Don't mind if I do, son." Silas gave a little bow. "But after you, Your Loveliness."

Belle grinned. She couldn't help it. So often, people were intimidated by her background. Not Silas McCade. "Why thank you, Silas." She led the way into a roomy two-story foyer. Wide stairs led to the upper floor. It seemed to her a sturdy, solid house. A house that could do with a woman's touch—some brighter colors, different curtains. But still, it was a fine house. Clean and well-maintained.

"Let's go in the living room." Preston helped her out of her coat and hung it on the hall tree, along with his own and that handsome cowboy hat he always wore. Then he gestured toward the open double door to her left. She went in. The McCade men followed. Marcus remained behind, near the front door. Preston told her, "Have a seat."

She did, on the sofa.

Silas took an easy chair across from her. "A little whiskey would be welcome, son. You, Belle?"

"Nothing right now, thank you."

Preston poured a drink, gave it to his father and sat down in the other easy chair.

Silas started talking. About how he had the foreman's cottage across the yard, about how it got lonely at the ranch on a cold winter night. "Nice," he said, "to have a little feminine company around this old place." He started in about the horses they raised. "Preston's good with horses and our breeding program is one of the best in the state. But

I'm what they call a natural. You heard about those horse whisperers? I can do them one better. I don't even have to whisper. A horse just naturally wants to please me. They know what I'm thinking and they do what I want them to do without me having to breathe a word."

Preston advised softly, "Don't let false modesty stand in your way, Dad."

"Never have. Never will." Silas drained the last of his drink and stood again. "Well, I guess I've monopolized the conversation enough for this evening." He gave a nod of his shining silver head. "Belle, it's been a delight to meet you."

"And to meet you, Silas."

Now Silas seemed almost shy. "You come back again. Anytime. Often."

"Thank you."

He left them.

Preston waited until the front door closed behind him. "No one quite like my dad."

"He's a charmer, definitely."

"For God's sake, don't ever tell *him* that. He's impossible to live with as it is."

"I doubt that. I'm guessing he's good company. And that the two of you get along quite well together."

Preston looked at her levelly then. "Yeah, you guessed right."

She thought of her cousin Charlotte, her companion, who was back at their lodgings, with Ben. She counted on Charlotte in so many ways. They'd been together for four years. And they did well together, she and Charlotte. She imagined that Preston's relationship with his father might be somewhat the same.

He was watching her.

She met and held his gaze. It was so easy to do, to look at him. And it felt...good. Warm and exciting to be here with him. She hadn't expected this. To be so attracted to him. As a rule, she was a down-to-earth, practical person, not prone to flirtations or easy infatuations.

It probably wasn't a good thing to be so taken with him, when you came right down it. It was hard enough to be calm and objective about the task before her without these sparks flashing back and forth between them.

He said, "You're so quiet, all of a sudden...."

"Sorry. Just...thinking."

"About?"

"I was..." *Tell him. Tell him now.* But her courage deserted her. "...wondering if you have this big house all to yourself?"

"I do. My dad moved across the yard when I got back from college. He said it was a fine thing that I wanted to work with him. But the house would be mine one day and I might as well lay claim to it. He said the smaller house suited him. Doris, our longtime housekeeper, used to live in. But she remarried last year and moved to her new husband's place. He's got five acres not far from here. She comes in Monday through Friday to clean—here and across the yard at the old man's place. She also cooks for us."

"How many hired men do you have here?"

"We keep two hands on year-round, and then hire at least two more in the spring. There's another house, the men's cabin, with a living area downstairs and an open sleeping loft that holds six beds."

She remembered. "The cabin near the barn?"

"That's right. Doris cooks for the hands, too, Monday through Friday. Weekends, we play the meals by ear. It works out fine."

He would need a full-time nanny. Ben would change his life completely. He had no idea....

In her mind's eye, she saw him, suddenly, sitting in

Anne's lap, his blond head tipped back to smile at her adoringly, in those last days before she grew too ill to sit up.

Anne.

A sudden, hard wave of loss rolled through her. Her stomach knotted, her throat clutched and tears welled. She swallowed them down, blinked the moisture away.

"Belle?" He was rising from his chair. "What happened? What did I say? What's wrong?"

She put out a hand. "No. Sit down. Please. It's…all right. *I'm* all right. Honestly."

He sank back to the chair. "Why don't I believe you?"

Tell him. Tell him now. She opened her mouth to break the news.

Chapter Three

But Belle's leaden tongue refused to form the words. She pressed her lips together over the silence.

Preston was watching her, looking concerned as he waited for her to explain what the matter was.

She got up and went over to the big window that looked out on the wide front porch. Outside, the sky was clear now. A light dusting of snow sparkled under the quarter moon. "The clouds are all gone. The sky is so beautiful, so thick with stars...."

"That's how it is in Montana. We're closer to heaven here." He said it so softly. And he was on his feet again. She heard him come toward her, his tread quiet but nonetheless charged with great energy, with purpose. He stopped close at her back. She felt his presence there acutely. A sense of that steadiness he possessed, of the density and power in his strong male body.

She turned to him, her breath snagging in her throat at the look in his eyes. So tender. So…intent.

How to tell him? How to say it? How to lead up gracefully to the moment when she handed over that final letter to him? It had been tucked within the letter Anne had written to Belle, in an envelope with his name on it. She hadn't opened the envelope. That wouldn't have been right. But she hoped whatever Anne had written to him, it might help him understand. She had it with her now, in the pocket of her skirt. All she had to do was bring it out, hand it over….

But then, really, maybe it was too soon. Maybe she should wait a little, give herself more time to…

To what? Any excuses she might have had not to tell him had dried up and blown away like dead leaves in the wind. She liked him. He seemed a fine man. His ranch looked to her like a good-size operation. The house was perfectly livable. And anyway, there would be plenty of money from Anne's estate. Even if Preston's personal finances were shaky—which they did not appear to be—Ben would never want for anything. His mother had left him everything she owned.

She opened her mouth to tell all.

And he said, "Tell you what. Let's go outside. I'll show you the stables and we can look at the stars without a window in the way."

Belle realized she'd been holding her breath and let it out slowly. "I would love to see the stables."

They put their coats and gloves back on and he took her outside. The icy snow crunched under the heels of their boots as they crossed the yard, past the barn to the stables, which were large and clean and well-maintained. He explained his breeding program and the supplemental lights that made the stable bright enough to read the small print of a newspaper even at that time of night. The point was to trick the mares' reproductive cycles into thinking it was spring come January. That way, the foals were born early the following year. And because all foals' official birthday of any given year was January 1, a foal born early had significant advantage over foals born later in the year when it came to competitive activities like racing.

His horses were healthy and beautiful. She admired his way with them, could see that he treated them well, noted the way they chuffed and nuzzled him, responding eagerly to the sound of his voice. She saw how they sought the touch of his hand.

"You're like my sister Alice," she said as they were leaving. They stood under the bright lights suspended from the ceiling beams, the smell of hay and horses all around them. "Her horses love her."

"I read about your sister."

"On the internet, you mean?"

He nodded. His eyebrows were burnished gold in the light from above. "I read that she raises Akhal-Tekes."

"Yes, she does."

"The most ancient breed on earth, a breed prized by Alexander the Great and Genghis Khan."

She was impressed. "You know the legend of the Tekes?"

"I know horses. The Nez Perce Indians are currently breeding them with Appaloosas, did you know that?" She did know, but she kept quiet, hoping he might continue. And he did. "It's an effort to replicate the legendary Nez Perce horse, which is believed to have originated from Akhal-Teke stock brought to the New World by Russian traders." He touched her hair, the lightest breath of a touch. "A Teke is a loyal horse," he said. "A sensitive, one-owner horse."

Belle watched his shadowed face so closely as he spoke. Why, oh why did she find it so difficult to tell him? Beneath the tough exterior he needed to make a life in such a rugged land, he truly was a fine man, a sensitive man. He would be a good father.

Her throat was tight again, her eyes brimming. Because she knew what held her back.

As soon as she told him, she would be out of time. Out of hope. Any faint dream she might have nourished in her secret heart that Ben could somehow stay with her...that dream was dying.

She didn't need to wait for any private investigator's detailed report. Just being around him had told her all that she needed to know. He was a good man and he had a father's rights. And once he knew, once he got over the shock and the disbelief that Anne had never said a word to him, never made any attempt to contact him after that one night they spent together, once he knew the truth at last, he would set about claiming what was his.

She was going to lose Ben as she had lost Anne. There was absolutely no doubt about it now. She had known from the moment Preston walked into the diner that morning. It was just taking her poor, battered heart a little while to catch up with her mind.

"Belle?" He looked stricken. "What did I say? I swear, I don't get it. Whatever it is, whatever you want from me, you only need to say it." He reached for her. She knew he would touch her tear-wet cheek.

"Don't." She shoved his hand away, swiped the traitorous tears from her face. "Please. I...let's go. Back to the house. We'll talk. I'll...explain."

He was silent. His expression changed, grew harder. Closed to her. He didn't understand.

But how could he? She'd told him nothing. Yet.

Unspeaking, they turned for the stable door. He pushed

it open for her. She went through, her head lowered, steps dragging. He followed, pausing, turning to secure the latch.

She was aware, for a moment, of the ever-present Marcus, silent and watchful in the shadows not far away. But only for a moment.

Because magic happened.

Magic happened and the crushing weight of her unhappiness, of her terrible obligation, of her loss—all of that was lifted. She raised her head and saw the miracle that waited overhead.

The sky was alive with melting, pulsing, vivid color. A concert of color.

"Preston…" She didn't even stop to think about the confusing mishmash of signals she was giving him. Automatically, she reached for his hand.

"The northern lights." He said it softly, with reverence, his gaze turned upward to the sky. And his warm, strong fingers closed around hers. The distance she'd put between them moments ago vanished. It was gone as though it had never been.

There was only pure beauty lighting the heavens. And the two of them, together, hand in hand, watching the wonder unfold.

Red, yellow, green, blue, a purple as deep as the heart of the night, a pink like the blush on the cheek of an angel, the colors moved and slid and dipped and danced across the giant canvas of the sky. Alive, rhythmic, majestic, otherworldly—perfect notes in a silent symphony.

Preston pulled her closer as they watched, until she stood tucked up against him, his arm around her shoulders. She didn't think to resist. Why should she resist? How often in a lifetime did magic like this occur? She'd been born in a palace, seen the wonders of the world. But a concert of pure color pulsing above her, filling the endless star-scattered darkness of the sky?

Never, until that night. Never in her life before.

How long did it last? Minutes only. Minutes that seemed to her sweetly, enchantingly, perfectly endless.

But then the brightness began to fade. She sighed when she saw the end coming after all. The bands of color were losing brightness and form. Much too soon, it would be over.

And he was gazing down at her. She saw the magic reflected in his eyes. He touched her chin, brushed that rough, warm hand across her cheek.

She didn't stop him. She couldn't, not right then. And even if she could have, she wouldn't have. She *wanted* what happened next.

He lowered his golden head. His fine lips touched hers. She sighed again and turned her body into him. It was wrong of her, and she knew it. But for that moment and that moment only, wisdom was silenced for the sake of a kiss.

For that moment, it was the most natural, the most *right* thing—to press her lips to his under the last pale and fading echoes of the aurora borealis.

And it was a beautiful kiss, as magical as the sight they had just witnessed together. She forgot everything—the bodyguard waiting close by, her duty to her lost friend, even the precious child she would soon have to surrender to him.

Finally, he lifted his head. He stared down at her, bemused. "Belle…" The way he said her name required no answer. He raised her hand to his mouth. She shivered at the touch of his lips. It wasn't with cold. "Come on. Inside…" He still had his arm wrapped around her. She let him hold her, let him guide her. Together they turned for the warmth of the house.

In the foyer, he took her coat. She gave it reluctantly.

She knew what came next and it was not going to grace-
ful or pleasant.

She turned to Marcus, who had followed them in. "Will
you wait in the car, please?"

Marcus frowned, but he did as she bade him. He went
out the front door, closing it quietly behind him.

Preston said nothing. He'd grown watchful again.

"Could we perhaps…sit down?" she asked, the words
carefully measured.

He gestured her ahead of him. They went into the living room. As before, she sat on the sofa, in the same spot
she'd taken earlier.

He offered, "Coffee, maybe?"

Perhaps a little false courage. "I don't suppose you have
any brandy?"

He went to the cabinet in the corner, got out a crystal
decanter and a proper brandy snifter. He poured her the
drink and brought it to her.

She thanked him and took a larger sip than she should
have. Brandy, after all, was meant to be savored. It burned
going down. And when it spread its warmth in her belly,
she felt no braver than she had before. She set the glass on
the low table in front of her.

He settled into the easy chair. "All right, hit me with it.
Why are you here in Elk Creek, Montana, at Christmastime, Belle?"

Where to start? "Do you…happen to remember a certain archaeology student named Anne Benton? She came
to Elk Creek three summers ago."

He frowned. "Why do you ask?"

"I'm getting there. I promise I am. But could you just…"
She sighed, shook her head. "*Do* you remember Anne?"

He stiffened. And he looked at her steadily for several awful seconds. But then he shrugged. "Sure I remember her. I liked her. Why?"

Pres had no idea why they were suddenly talking about Anne Benton.

He'd hardly known the woman, though he had liked her. She'd told him she was getting a doctorate in anthropology. A couple of times he'd gone riding out near the caves where she and the others in her group were working, cataloging the artifacts and pictographs in the caves, they said. Pres would stop. Visit a little with them—and with Anne especially. He remembered she was friendly, with an easy, open way about her.

It hadn't been anything romantic. He'd just liked her, that was all.

He'd rested his elbows on the chair arms, his hands folded between. He looked down at them. "I...spent an evening with her once, just before she left town." He hadn't realized he would say that out loud until he heard the words coming out of his mouth.

"Spent an evening?" Belle prompted softly.

Pres didn't like this. Not one bit. *He* ought to be the one asking the questions—and *she* should be coming up with the answers.

But somehow, she brought out the truth in him. She made him want to open up to her, to tell her all the things he'd never told a living soul. "It was a bad time for me that summer. I was going to get married. My fiancée dumped me for another guy."

Belle made a low sound, of sympathy. "Oh, Preston..."

He went on, "She married that other guy on the second Saturday in September, which was right at the end of Anne's stay in Elk Creek. I ran into Anne that night, at a certain roadhouse not far from town."

Belle drew in a slow, careful breath. "You were with Anne on the night your fiancée married another man?"

"That's right. I was trying to drown my sorrows. Anne was with her scientist friends, celebrating the end of their dig. She was drinking, too. Almost as heavily as I was. I'm ashamed to say, I drank enough that my memory of that night is pretty much a blur. I didn't go home. I wasn't safe to drive. I got a room in the motel adjacent to the road-house. I think I remember Anne being there, in the motel room, with me. But maybe I just imagined that."

"Imagined it?" Belle was frowning.

He raised both big hands, palms up. "I don't know. I know that when I woke up in the morning, there was no sign of her and I was alone. I pulled myself together and came home."

Belle studied his face. She seemed to be looking for answers there.

He had no answers. And what in the hell was this all about anyway? It was time—well *past* time—she came out with it. "I think I've said enough, a damn sight more than enough. And you've told me nothing. What's Anne Benton got to do with anything? Are you telling me you know her? Did she mention me or something?"

"Oh, Preston. Yes. Yes...."

"What? Yes, you know her? Yes, she mentioned me?"

"I...both. Anne has been my dearest friend in all the world. We met at Duke University. She was getting her undergraduate degree and I was studying nursing. She had no extended family, but her parents had been wealthy. They adored her. She was their only child and she never wanted for anything. Her father died when she was eight. And her mother raised her alone—and then died the year Anne graduated from high school. She was on her own in life by the time I met her. And I was far from home. She and I...we became like sisters."

He still didn't get it. What did any of this have to do with him? "What are you saying? Anne wants to talk to me, is that it?"

"I...oh, I really am trying to explain. I'm not doing a very good job and I realize that..."

He felt that need again, the one he seemed to have around her—to go to her, to hold her, soothe her, tell her that everything was going to be all right.

How could he tell her that? He didn't know that. He was the one in the dark here. "Just go ahead, okay? Just... continue."

"Oh, sweet Lord..." She pressed the back of her hand to her mouth, steadied herself, lowered it. "I'm sorry to tell you, so sorry. Not long ago, Anne was diagnosed with ALL—acute lymphocytic leukemia. I went to her, took care of her, but she didn't make it."

He tried to wrap his mind around that one. "You're telling me that Anne is dead?"

She swallowed, convulsively. Her eyes brimmed. She shook her head, blinked the tears away. "Yes. She died ten days ago."

"My God." It seemed impossible. "She was such a great woman. So young, so full of life..."

"Yes. And she...had a little boy. His name is Benjamin. He's eighteen months old."

Pres remembered. "The boy folks in town say you brought with you to Elk Creek?" He watched her head bob with her swift nod. She swallowed hard again. And right then, as he stared into her wide, wounded eyes, he made the connection. He raised both hands, palms out, shook his head. "Wait a minute. I still don't even know for certain if she...if we..."

"*I* know." Belle's voice had gained strength again. She spoke firmly now. "Anne would never claim you were Ben's father if she didn't know beyond a doubt that you were. She named me his legal guardian. She knew I would always take care of him and that I would give him all the love in my heart and an excellent start in life. She also knew she should have contacted you. She realized that both you and Ben deserve to know each other, that Ben needs his father and you have a right and a duty to be with your son. So she set me the task of making that happen."

Pres was not keeping up with this flood of information. He was still stuck back there with the fact that, apparently, he actually did have sex with Anne Benton on the night that Lucy married Monty Polk. "Damn it to hell. If it happened, it was only one night."

Beautiful Belle gave him a sad little smile. "Sometimes one night is all it takes."

"Dear God." He realized he was on his feet. And his knees didn't want to hold him up. He sank to the chair again. "A boy. A little boy…Ben, you said? His name is Ben?"

"Yes. Ben." Belle produced an envelope from the pocket of her skirt. Her hands were shaking. "She gave this to me two days before she died. It was tucked inside a note she wrote to me. She told me to…" The tears welled again. She pressed her lips together, forced herself to go on. "…to read the note addressed to me after she was gone. That note told me who you were and where to find you. Also in that note, she asked that I give you this." She extended the envelope across the coffee table toward him.

He took it from her trembling fingers. Struck with a sense of complete unreality, he tapped the end on the table, tore off the other end and removed the single sheet of folded paper within. He unfolded the thing, stared down at the words on it, words written in a hand that didn't appear to have been all that steady. Those words ran together at first, kind of wiggling, like a caravan of ants trudging without direction across the paper, refusing to take any recognizable form. With effort, he read it through once.

And then again.

And finally, on the third time through, the ragged writing made sense to him.

He dropped the letter onto the coffee table and tossed the envelope on top of it. And then he made himself speak, although his voice sounded rough, ill-used, raggedy as Anne Benton's handwriting. "She says the boy is mine. She says she woke up in that motel by the roadhouse with me and… she didn't know what she would say to me. So she just… left. She says when she found out she was having my baby, she didn't know how to tell me. She kept meaning to do it, but she never managed to work up the courage."

Belle was nodding again. "She told me she always intended to get in touch with you, to tell you…"

"But she didn't." How could she not? How could she keep the reality of his own child from him? It wasn't right. For the first time since he'd met the princess across from him, he felt the heat of anger in his veins, the blood pumping in furious spurts. Wrong. All wrong, what Anne Benton had done. "By God, she *didn't* come to me, didn't *tell* me.…"

Belle stood up. He stiffened in the chair and watched her warily as she came around the coffee table to his side. Gingerly, she touched his shoulder. "Preston, please… Try to understand…"

He jerked free of her hand and glared up at her dead on. "I want you to go."

Belle longed to stay, to soothe him, to ease his confusion and frustration—and perhaps even to come to an agreement about how they would proceed from there. She had plans, detailed plans. She knew what to do and was prepared to move forward.

But she understood that she couldn't force him. He would need time to process such momentous news.

Plus, there was the way she'd handled telling him the situation: badly. She should have told him sooner—and she should have done a better job of it. So far, she'd mucked everything up, taking forever to get to the point, finding endless excuses to put off the inevitable.

And kissing him. What had possessed her to think that it would be all right to kiss him? It wasn't. It was wrong.

So very wrong. She'd…completely misled him. Indulged herself in an impossible romantic fantasy when she should have kept her focus on the important information Anne had trusted her to deliver with a certain delicacy and tact.

Of course he was angry. With Anne. *And* with her.

"Please go." He wasn't even looking at her. He had his elbows on his knees and his head in his hands. "Go now."

She thought again of all the things she still had to say to him. And then she reminded herself that none of those things had to be said that night. The least she could do after botching her first task here so completely was to leave the poor man alone to deal privately with the life-altering information she'd finally managed to deliver to him.

She turned for the foyer, where she took her coat off the hall tree and put it on. She pulled her gloves from the pocket and put them on, too. Then, quietly, she left through the front door, closing it gently behind her.

Out in the snow-dusted driveway, Marcus was waiting. He had the SUV's engine idling, ready to go. He got out when he saw her emerge from the house and opened the door to the backseat for her.

She ran down the front steps, pausing only for one brief

second to glance up at the star-thick indigo bowl of the sky, hoping to see a last echo of the northern lights.

But there was nothing and that made her sad, made her feel as though the magic had never been.

Pounding sounds invaded her dreams.

Belle struggled up through dragging layers of sleep, groaning. The room was dark. The time glowed at her from the bedside clock: 6:14 a.m.

More pounding—on the door that led out to the landing. What in the…

In the crib across the room, Ben woke with a startled cry. He began calling for Anne. "Mama! Mama!"

Belle flicked on the lamp, threw back the covers, pulled on her robe and went to him. The pounding continued.

"Mama!" Ben cried.

She scooped his warm, plump body up into her arms and hugged him close.

Ben pushed at her with his little fists and kept crying. "Mama! Mama…"

Outside, she heard Preston's voice, followed by another that sounded like Silas. She held on to Ben, stroking his back, rocking him from side to side, kissing his forehead, whispering, "Shh, shh, now. It's all right, sweetheart. It's all right…" as he continued to wail and push her away. Outside, there were scuffling noises. Someone fell heavily against the door.

The startling sound brought another frightened cry from Ben. Then he grabbed on to her, buried his face against her neck and sobbed, "Mama, Mama…" The words broke her heart. And his plaintive, lonely little cries made her feel powerless and useless and somehow cruel—to deny this perfect, beautiful child what he needed most of all. He shook his head against her neck, his hot tears smearing on her skin at the same time as he pressed himself so close against her, needing comfort so desperately, he grabbed for her even as he cried for the one he really wanted.

"Darling, shh. It's all right. You're all right...." She pressed her lips to his fine blond hair, breathed in the baby smell of him, milky and warm, a scent like fresh bread and baby lotion enchantingly combined.

"Mama, Mama..." He let out a garbled string of sad little nonsense words.

"Shh, Mama loves you. She loves you so much. But she can't come," she whispered against skin. "I'm here, though. I have you. You're safe, you're all right...."

Outside, the scuffling sounds continued. Again, something heavy bounced against the door.

And then she heard her cousin Charlotte's sharp voice. "Stop this. Stop it this instant."

A few more thuds and grunts followed.

And then she clearly heard Silas McCade say, "You damn fool, get hold of yourself."

After that, there was silence from outside at last.

Charlotte spoke again, more quietly. Belle couldn't make out the words. Then a door shut.

A moment later, Charlotte tapped on the door that joined their rooms. Ben had stopped wailing. He had his head buried in the crook of her neck and he was sniffling dejectedly, his little body shuddering in the aftermath of his tears.

She carried him to the inner door, rubbing his back, her lips to his temple as she went. When she reached the door, she settled the baby a little higher on her shoulder and turned the lock to admit her cousin, companion and dear friend.

"The...father has arrived," Charlotte said, her prominent gray-green eyes wider than ever. She clutched the high neck of her ruffled robe with one hand and held the other hand around her middle.

"I heard," said Belle.

"He wants to see Ben. He and Marcus had a bit of an altercation. They're waiting outside with a loud-mouthed older fellow whom I'm assuming is the grandfather."

"Has he been drinking?" Belle asked.

Charlotte frowned. "Which one?"

"Preston—but when you come right down to it, have *either* Preston or his father been drinking?"

Charlotte thought it over. Finally, she decided, "I don't believe so. I think it was a case of the blood running high, as it were. They both appear sober and I didn't smell liquor on either of them."

"Very well." Belle kissed Ben's velvety cheek. He had his fist in his mouth by then. With a final hiccup and a weary little sigh, he laid his head on her shoulder. "Tell Preston we will meet him…where? It's so early. I have no idea."

"The restaurant across the street should be open," Charlotte said. "I checked the hours yesterday. Six in the morning until eight in the evening."

"Wonderful," Belle said wearily. Maybe fortune would smile on them and the restaurant would be empty at this hour, giving them all a little privacy to deal with this difficult situation. "Tell them the diner, then. We'll meet them there in twenty minutes."

Chapter Four

Belle, Charlotte and Ben entered the Sweet Stop together. Ben was bundled up and tucked in his stroller. The ever-present Marcus, sporting a black eye, followed close behind them. The diner was far from empty. Apparently, many of the good citizens of Elk Creek took breakfast before dawn. As had happened the day before, a hush fell over the establishment when Belle and the others came in. People paused with their coffee mugs halfway to their lips and stared.

Preston and Silas had taken a back booth and were waiting for them. One of them must have thought to ask for a high chair. It stood at the end of the booth. Preston, who faced the door, had a swollen lower lip and a small cut above his right eye. His gaze locked with Belle's for a too-brief moment. An echo of last night's magic arced between them.

And then was gone.

He and Silas both stood up as Belle, pushing Ben's

stroller, came toward them, Charlotte at her side. Marcus hung back near the door.

Belle reached the men looming by the booth. She moved around to the side of the stroller to take care of Ben and suggested over her shoulder, "If you two gentlemen wouldn't mind sitting in the inner seats? Charlotte and I need to be next to the high chair for Ben."

Neither of the McCade men answered. She glanced over at them. Neither had moved either. Both of them stood stock-still, wearing identical expressions of dumbstruck wonder, staring down at the child in the stroller.

Ben, bundled up in blankets and a miniature down jacket, a blue wool hat over his white-blond hair, gazed solemnly back at them.

Charlotte broke the silence. "Ahem. Sit down, please." She made a shooing motion with both slim hands. "Sit down and slide over. Both of you."

That seemed to break the spell. The men sat and slid to the window side of the booth. Charlotte hung up her heavy coat and took the remaining seat on Silas's side of the table. Belle got Ben out of his warm hat and fat coat.

When she eased him into the high chair, he smiled up at her, sweet as any angel, his earlier misery completely forgotten. "Belle. Eat!" He pounded his hands flat on the chair tray—but not too hard. Just enough to punctuate his excitement at the thrilling prospect of breakfast. He loosed a happy string of nonsense noises.

She laughed low as she took off her coat. It was so good to see him back to his cheerful little self again. "Yes, Benjamin. We shall eat." She gave him a biscuit to keep him occupied until his meal arrived and then took the seat next to Preston, who wore a winter-green corduroy shirt and a look both stern and completely stunned.

The waitress from yesterday, Selma, arrived with a coffeepot and an order pad. She poured coffee for all of them. Belle and Charlotte ordered.

Selma glanced at Silas and then at Preston. Both of them said, "The usual."

The meal was a strange one, which really wasn't all that surprising under the circumstances. Charlotte bravely tried to contribute something resembling conversation. She spoke of the weather and of the beauty and majesty of the local forests and mountains. Belle agreed with her companion that Montana was wild and rugged and beautiful. Charlotte had purchased a copy of the most recent edition of the *Elk Creek Gazette.* She'd read about the various holiday events that were coming up in the next few weeks.

"If we're still here, we must attend the craft fair," she said.

Belle agreed that, indeed, they must.

Preston methodically shoveled in food. He had nothing to say. Neither did the previously talkative Silas. Both men continued to seem astounded by Ben. They would glance in the child's direction and then blink and gape. After a moment or two, they would catch themselves at it and resolutely return to devouring the enormous breakfasts they'd ordered.

Ben watched the two rugged ranchers warily at first. But then, after fifteen minutes or so, he seemed to realize that they presented no threat to him. He grew accustomed to their staring and he ignored them. He ate his cereal and fruit with gusto and drank watered-down apple juice from the sippy cup Belle carried along wherever they went.

There was so very much to discuss. But every time she glanced at Preston's battered face and saw his blank-eyed expression, she realized she didn't know where to start. And even if she had known what to say, the busy diner didn't seem the right place to talk. So she said nothing—

except to agree with Charlotte that the scenery in Montana was spectacular and she would love to visit the Christmas Craft Fair.

When the meal was finally over, Preston claimed the check, piled some bills on top of it and cleared his throat. "Belle, I'd like a few words. Alone." Grudgingly, he added, "Please."

She took a wet wipe from a pocket of Ben's diaper bag and cleaned the little sweetheart's face and hands. "Charlotte, could you take Ben back across the street with you?"

"Of course."

"Thank you." She faced Preston again. "How about a stroll?"

"Fine."

Charlotte rose, put on her coat and scooped Ben out of the high chair. She put him in the stroller and bundled him up again.

He laughed, a delighted chortling sound that warmed Belle's heart. "Shar-Shar. Kiss."

"Oh, yes." Charlotte leaned close to him and he made a loud smacking sound with his little mouth against her cheek. She beamed at him. "Thank you, young man—now let's put on this nice, warm hat." She put it on him and tied the yarn ribbons under his chin. "There. Are we ready?"

"Yes!" declared Ben.

"Bundle up," she instructed Belle in that motherly way she sometimes did as she got behind the stroller and aimed it at the door. "It's bitterly cold out there."

"I will," Belle promised.

Marcus opened the door when Charlotte reached it. She pushed the stroller through. Wordless, Preston and Silas watched them go.

And then, out of nowhere, Silas found his voice. "That boy's a McCade if I ever saw one." He said it loud enough that every listening ear in the diner was treated to the big news. And then he spoke to Preston. "And damned if he didn't get those baby blue eyes of yours."

"Keep it down, Dad," Preston growled, already on his feet. He shrugged into his sheepskin coat and shoved his hat on his head. Then he grabbed Belle's coat and held it open for her. "Belle."

She got up and let him help her into it. "Thank you."

Silas was sliding from the booth.

Preston stopped him. "You stay here, Dad. Have yourself to another cup of coffee. This won't take long."

"I'm up to my eyeballs in caffeine as it is," Silas grumbled. But he did sit back down.

"After you," said Preston.

She led the way to the door.

Outside, the gray sky was growing lighter. She pulled on her winter gloves and put on her wool hat against the blustery cold. With Marcus in their wake, they hunched down into their coat collars and forged off up the street, snowflakes whirling around them. Christmas decorations, battered by the harsh wind, clinked rhythmically against the Victorian-style streetlights that lined the street.

"I would like to…apologize," he said stiffly as they passed a jewelry store and then a gift shop, neither of which were open at that hour. "I got completely out of hand this morning at the motel."

She sent him a sideways glance. He had his head hunched very low and his hat tipped down against the wind, shadowing his eyes. His swollen mouth had a grim twist to it. In spite of the fact that he was going to take Ben from her, she felt a tug of sympathy. "I imagine it must be a lot to take in."

"Yeah, it is—and I shouldn't have been so hard on you

last night. You're only the messenger, right?" He laid on the irony.

That got her back up a little. "I am, as a matter of fact, Ben's legal guardian. So my responsibilities in this matter far exceed those of one who merely bears news."

"Fancy talk," he muttered.

"It happens to be the truth."

He made a low, scoffing sound. "Here's a truth for you. He's *my* son."

"I know that, Preston." She kept her voice carefully even.

"And he's what—a year and a half old?"

"Yes, he is."

"But this morning is the first time I've ever laid eyes on him. *That's* the truth. And it's not right." He waited—apparently for her to say something, to argue the point. When she didn't, he added, "She should have told me."

"I know. And *she* knew it, too. I don't know why she didn't get in touch with you before she—" it was still hard to say the words "—before she died. After college, we didn't see each other as often as we might have wished. She had her work. I had mine. I lived in Montedoro and traveled a great deal, raising funds and awareness for Nurses Without Boundaries. She was living here, in America—in Raleigh, North Carolina, and often off on a dig somewhere for her studies. I hadn't seen her in person for two years when she called to tell me she was sick."

"You'd never seen Ben until then?"

"No. I kept meaning to go to her, to meet her new baby, to spend some time catching up. But somehow, I never managed to make the time. Not until she called and told me about her illness, about how bad it was. I went to her then, at the end of October. We were with her until the

end, Charlotte and I. I asked her more than once about…
the baby's father."

He did look at her then. His eyes were haunted beneath
the brim of his hat. "This way." He offered his hand. She
took it and couldn't help thinking of the night before when
he had kissed her, when he had raised her hand to his
warm lips.

He led her off the sidewalk, into a courtyard between
the buildings, out of the wind. He let go of her fingers to
brush snow off one of the benches there. They sat down,
side-by-side but not touching.

He asked, "What did she say, when you asked her about
Ben's dad?"

"That it was a one-night thing. That she hardly knew
the man. And that she kept meaning to get in touch with
him. That she *would* get in touch with him—with *you,*
as it turned out. But she did nothing to make that happen
through her final month of life. When she gave me that
letter I showed you last night, I was reasonably certain of
what would be in it. By then, I had a good idea of what
she intended. I understood that she wasn't planning to be
the one to get in touch with the father of her child. I accepted that. I couldn't do otherwise. She was so sick. She
was in no condition to reach out to you, to tell you what
you needed to know."

"But there *was* plenty of time before she got sick for her
to have done the right thing. Why didn't she?"

"You would have to ask her that question."

"That would be a little difficult at this point."

She folded her hands and lowered her head. "Yes, it
would."

He was silent for a moment. He stared at the brick wall
opposite the bench where they sat. Then he asked, "Be-

fore that letter, she never told you my name or anything about me?"

Belle shivered, folded her arms around herself and shook her head. "No. Didn't I already say that?"

"I just want to get real clear on all this."

"She asked me not to read the letter until after she was gone. I did what she asked. I did it her way. It wasn't an easy time. My main concern was for my friend, to help her get through the final days of her life. The only other thing that mattered then was Ben—to make that horrible time as bearable for him as I possibly could, to make certain he knew that he was loved and safe and would always be cared for."

There was a moment. He stared straight ahead. She feared he would say something angry and hurtful. But he surprised her. In the end, he leaned toward her, bumping his shoulder against hers in way that struck her as reluctantly companionable. "Okay," he said. "I'm sorry. I am. I know this isn't your fault, that you're doing the best you can here. I'm sorry you lost your friend. I'm furious at Anne, but I still can't believe that she's…no longer on this earth. It's awful that she died. But the hard truth is that I've been a father for a year and a half and I just found out yesterday that I have a son. I want someone to blame for that and you're way too damn convenient."

"Yes," she said softly. "I can see that."

He stared at that brick wall some more. "She died less than two weeks ago, you said?"

"Yes."

"I gotta hand it to you." His voice was rough with carefully contained emotion. "You got here fast."

"There seemed…no excuse to put it off. Though I must confess, Preston, I wanted *only* to put it off, to take Ben home with me to Montedoro and bring him up as my own."

"But you couldn't. *You* did the right thing."

She turned toward him on the bench. "Please. She's gone. Don't hate her. She did the best she could. And she was Ben's mother. Don't…poison her memory for him."

He was looking in her eyes now. His mouth was grim, but his gaze was warmer than before. "I would never do that."

She did reach out then. She laid her hand on his arm. Beneath the sleeve of his coat, she felt the strength of him, that steadiness she'd admired from the first. "Good. I didn't think you would."

He looked down at her hand. She withdrew it. He said, "It was wrong what she did. I don't think I'll ever get over that. But that's not something the child has to know about. From what you're describing, she was a good mother. A loving mother."

"Oh, yes. She was."

"I'll, uh, focus on that."

"I'm grateful that you will." She wished she could make him truly understand the good, generous heart of her lost friend. But she didn't really understand herself why Anne hadn't done the right thing concerning her child's father. She put her hands between her knees, rubbed them together—and gave it one more shot. "Anne was…so independent. She never wanted to be tied down. She had her work that she loved. I don't think she ever planned to marry. And when she got pregnant with Ben… I don't know. She was happy to be having a baby. She told me so more than once, when we would speak on the phone. And then after Ben was born, I could hear the joy in her voice every time she mentioned her baby. But she still had no desire to have a husband, to make the traditional sort of family."

His jaw was set, his mouth a hard line. "None of that's an excuse for keeping him from me. You know that, right?"

She swallowed, hard. "Yes. Yes, I do."

"So let's leave it at that."

"All right. Let's." She sighed. "Please."

The fitful snow had stopped for the moment. It was fully light now. She tipped her head back, stared up at the slice of gray sky between the buildings.

He spoke again. "I want my son."

The four words landed like blows. Yes, she had expected them. But that didn't make them any less painful to hear. She thought of Ben, that morning, crying his heart out, his soft little face pressed into her neck, his tears on her skin. "I understand."

"You're saying you'll give him to me, then?"

"That is my intention. Eventually."

"Eventually. I'm not sure I like that word."

She turned toward him on the bench and she looked at him squarely. "As I said, I am his legal guardian."

His eyes blazed blue fire. "You can't keep my son from me. I'll take you to—"

She cut him off with a wave of her hand. "Please, no threats. It hurts me, more than you will ever know, to be losing him. But more important than my pain or your needs as a father, more important than anything else, is that we do right by Ben. Surely you agree with that."

"Of course I do."

"I think we can avoid an ugly legal battle. I think we can…do better than that."

He looked away, tipping his head down, touching the brim of his hat, and then he sat tall and faced her once more. "You have some kind of plan?"

"As a matter of fact, I do."

"Tell me, then."

"First, the paternity test."

"I don't need a damn test to know my own son."

"Of course you don't. But why not establish your paternity in the eyes of the law from the start? Might as well clear up any doubts now. I've already contacted a lab in Missoula. We can go today, if that's possible for you. It's a simple procedure. They take a buccal swab from inside the cheek. The test will be conducted under a strict chain of evidence. That way, the fact that you are Ben's biological father can be established legally beyond any doubt."

He seemed wary, but not altogether unwilling. "How long do we have to wait for the results?"

"If the test is done today, we should have results by early next week."

"Next week," he echoed, as though turning her answer over in his mind, checking it for flaws.

"That's right, and in the meantime, do you, er, think you have room for us at the ranch?"

Belle's question took Pres by surprise. With considerable cautiousness, he asked, "Room for whom, exactly?"

"Ben, Charlotte, Marcus and me."

She expected to move into his house? "Why?"

Her soft mouth trembled a little. He could see this wasn't any easier for her than it was for him. "Ben needs time. Surely you can understand that Charlotte and I can't just drop him off at your house and go home to Montedoro?"

It was so strange. His life had been feeling pretty meaningless, a little empty, since the whole thing went to hell with Lucy. But now that he'd seen the child, now that he knew absolutely that the boy was his, he felt energized. Focused. He didn't have a wife, but he did have a child. "I want him. He's mine and I will learn to take care of him."

She reached out as if to touch his arm again, then thought better of it. She pulled her hand back, slid it between her knees with its mate, hunching her shoulders a little, hoarding her body heat. "Please, Preston. Consider. Ben's already lost the one constant in his life up till now, his mother. He counts on me, and on Charlotte. It could be terribly damaging for him if we were to just…disappear. He will need time, to get to know you and your father, to come to love you, to transfer his trust to you. Plus, even though your house is solid and comfortable and you're clearly willing to take on the care of a small child, it won't hurt you to have a little help at the start."

A little help at the start…

He supposed she had a point.

His head was spinning and his life felt strangely cracked wide-open all of a sudden. He had a son. Belle would be staying with him. Her companion, Charlotte, too. *And* the damn bodyguard.

He touched his lip. Still swollen. He could do without the bodyguard. But he understood that Marcus went where Belle went. Plus, well, he knew she was right. His son needed time to become accustomed to his new life, to his father and grandfather, who would care for him now.

"How long will you be staying?" he asked.

She was shivering. She wrapped her arms around herself, rubbed them to warm herself a little. "I don't know. I thought we could play it by ear, see how it goes. A month, I would guess, in any case." Her fine, aristocratic nose was bright red. Her lips—those lips he had tasted only last night—were just a little bit blue. Her breath plumed in the icy air. "Until the New Year?"

He rose, tipped his head in the direction of the sidewalk. "Come on. You're freezing. Let's get back."

She looked up at him through those amazing golden eyes, but she didn't stand. "Just tell me. Are you willing?"

Are you willing? The question seemed to echo in his head.

Okay, he was still pretty ticked off at Anne Benton.

She'd had his baby and never said a damn word about it to him. But Anne was gone forever. And as for Belle, well, he had to give her credit. She was a hell of a woman, a woman who was only trying to do the right thing.

The hard fact was, he had no idea how to take care of a kid. But he wanted the boy. Absolutely. More than he wanted to draw his next breath.

The world, for him, so bleak and without potential since Lucy dumped him, was suddenly full of strange and terrifying promise.

"I'm willing," he told her, and reached down his hand. "We'll do it your way."

Chapter Five

Pres got his first lesson in child care that day. He learned how to properly attach a car seat into the backseat of his quad cab. The seat went in facing the rear.

He and Belle got into a little wrangle about that. Because, come on, why shouldn't the kid face front and get a decent view of what was going on?

She patiently explained that it was safest for a child to ride rear-facing until the age of two. "Their vulnerable heads and necks are much better protected that way in the event of a crash."

"I'm not going to crash," he informed her.

She folded her arms across her middle. "Spoken like a man." And then she won out by reminding him that he had promised to be guided by her. "Plus, it's only six more months, then he'll be facing front. The time will fly by. Believe me."

That stopped him. Six months. By then, Belle would

be long gone. Ben would be calling him Daddy. His world was changing in a very big way. His life would never be the same.

"All right." He studied the installation pictures on the side of the car seat. "I'm on it." It wasn't that hard. He had it hooked in and properly secured in no time.

She checked his work. "Very good." She signaled Charlotte, who was waiting with Ben and the old man in the warmth of the motel reception room.

Belle's companion came out carrying the boy. The old man pushed the empty stroller, which he folded up and stuck under the camper shell in the back without even having to be told to do it. Like he knew exactly what to do with all the equipment you needed to take care of a kid.

And maybe he did, come to think of it. He'd raised Pres after all.

Charlotte marched right up to Pres. "Excellent job installing the seat."

"Er, thank you, ma'am."

Ben was making chortling sounds and trying to stick his mittened fingers into Charlotte's mouth. "Shar-Shar…" He said something else. Something not in any language Pres was familiar with.

Charlotte kissed his cheek. "Yes, and I adore you, too, young man." She caught Belle's eye and the two women exchanged a look. Then Charlotte said, "And for your next lesson, you will be putting him in the seat." He realized she was talking to him when she tried to hand the kid over to him. Panic gripped him.

The boy didn't seem to like the idea either. He let out a scared little squeak and buried his head against the older woman's shoulder. "No. Shar-Shar. No…"

He felt the strangest admixture of relief and disappointment. "Uh, maybe we ought to give him a chance to get used to me first...."

Charlotte regarded him through those enormous eyes of hers. "Put your hand on his back. Gently." He was afraid to do it. What if the kid started crying or something? It would be his fault. "Do it," Belle's companion said pleasantly, yet with a definite thread of steel underneath.

So he did it. He laid his gloved hand lightly on the small back of the little boy. Even through the layers of winter clothing, he felt the kid's living warmth.

Ben lifted his head and looked over his shoulder. It was a wary sort of look, but at least he didn't look scared or like he was about to burst into tears.

"Hi," Pres said, for lack of anything better. He felt like an idiot. And at the same time, pretty damn wonderful.

"Hi," the boy parroted in a small voice. And then he pressed his face into Charlotte's shoulder again, his small arms clutching tightly around her neck.

Pres arched an eyebrow at Belle's companion. Charlotte gave him a regal nod, which he took as permission to remove his hand. He did, slowly. With great care.

Charlotte put the boy in the car seat. They headed for Missoula, Pres and Belle in front, Charlotte with the little one in back. The old man rode with the bodyguard in the black SUV.

The paternity test didn't take long. There were forms to fill out, IDs to produce. Pres let them take his thumbprint. For Ben, they wanted a print of his right foot. And they took pictures of both of them as well. Then a nurse swiped a Q-tip along the inside of his cheek. She did the same to Ben. The results would be sent to the ranch by courier at the beginning of the following week.

That was it. It wasn't even lunchtime yet, so they went

straight back to Elk Creek and had lunch at the Sweet Stop in the same booth they'd shared that morning.

After that, Belle checked out of the Drop On Inn. Larry was running the front desk. He fell all over himself saying how sorry he was to see them go and how much he hoped they'd enjoyed their stay. Pres wanted to tell the fool to cool his jets, but he kept his mouth shut about it. It wasn't his business if Larry Seabuck wanted to act like a love-addled fool. And Belle knew how to handle herself. She nodded and smiled and thanked Larry for his hospitality.

Outside, his father and the bodyguard were loading up the SUV and the back of the quad cab with suitcases and baby equipment. Pres went out to help, although they were doing just fine without him. It was better than watching Larry drool all over Belle.

For the ride to the ranch, somehow Charlotte ended up in the backseat of the SUV with the old man. The car seat was already in Pres's truck, so Belle put Ben into it. Pres assumed she'd be riding in the back with him.

But she took the other seat in front. She buckled herself in and sent him a companionable glance. Her eyes were shining. Like they were on some grand adventure together.

He couldn't help giving her a smile. Maybe he was as bad as Larry, when you came right down to it. One look from those amber eyes of hers and he was a goner. He knew he needed to watch himself.

She was here to help him become a father to his son. And then she would go back to her country on the coast of France, back to living in a palace and jetting around the world to disadvantaged countries, where her mere presence brought funds for much-needed medical supplies and raised awareness of people struggling and in need.

Her smooth brows drew together. "Preston, is there something the matter?"

"Not a thing," he baldly lied. "Ready?"

She nodded. "Let's go."

He put the truck in gear and off they went.

"'Scuse us, Belle."

"Oops." She stepped clear of the doorway. Preston's father and Marcus came in, carrying Ben's crib between them. She pointed. "How about on that wall?"

They carried the crib over there, extended and locked the legs and then left again to get the rest.

Belle lingered. The upstairs room was nice and large with a couple of big windows to let in plenty of light. It was one door down from the master suite where Preston slept and there was another bedroom on the other side. Belle planned to take that room for the next month.

There was a child's desk in the corner, a bookcase and two full-size chests of drawers. And a single bed with a brown bedspread. The walls were covered in faded green-and-white stripes and the curtains were of a dull brown. The room could be perfect for a little boy—with some paint. And some new curtains and blinds. And maybe some wall stenciling or even a mural.

Preston came in with the collapsible changing table. "Where?"

She pointed. "There."

He put it where she'd indicated and opened it up. "How's that?"

"Wonderful."

He was watching her. "Then why are you frowning?"

"The bed needs to go. And I have to start making a list of everything else that needs doing in here."

"Hey." He raked his hand back through his thick golden-brown hair. "That was *my* bed when I was a kid."

"You can bring it back in when Ben is ready for it."

"And when will that be?" he asked.

Outside, the sky had cleared again. Thin winter sun slanted in the window near where he stood. It brought out more of the gold in his hair. His shoulders went on for days. And it wasn't only that she liked looking at him. He was a fine man, in his heart, where it mattered, someone who would always do the right thing.

A wry smile curved his lips. "You are a thousand miles away."

She shook herself. "No, I am right here, in this nice, big room that cries out for fresh paint and new curtains."

He folded his strong arms across his broad chest and gave the room a once-over. Slowly. "Okay, you may have a point."

"Good. It's so nice when we see eye to eye."

He laughed. It was a slightly rusty sound, as though he didn't laugh often. "I think that's my job, isn't it? To make sure I see eye-to-eye with you on all things Ben-related."

She mirrored his pose, folding her own arms across her middle. "It shouldn't be difficult. Because I know whereof I speak."

"I love the way you talk. *Whereof.* Nobody uses whereof anymore."

A little shiver went through her. Because of the light in his eyes and the teasing curve of his mouth. "Oh, yes, they do. *I* just used it."

"You didn't answer my question about the bed. When will Ben be ready for a real bed?"

"Soon. Six months. A year, perhaps…"

"How about this? We leave the bed here. He gets used to having it around. Maybe he sees that other people sleep in beds instead of cribs. Maybe he gets interested in sleeping in a bed himself."

It was her turn to laugh. "He's a year and a half old, Preston. He can't even form a coherent sentence yet."

"But he will. Soon. And when he's ready, the bed will be ready for him."

She looked at him obliquely. "How can I possibly argue with such clear and cogent reasoning?"

"Clear and cogent. That's me, all the way." He looked very pleased with himself. "So the bed stays?"

She gave the bed a disapproving glance. "It cries out for new bedding."

"Fine. We'll get a new bedspread. Sheets, all that. But the bed stays?"

"All right."

"Good."

They looked at each other, neither speaking. She thought about kissing him, about how very much she had *liked* kissing him.

And then she thought how she never *should* have kissed him, how kissing him had only confused the issue, made it more difficult to tell him about Ben, and probably increased his animosity when she finally did tell him. It had been touch and go between them—last night and this morning.

Things were going better now. She'd be well advised not to do anything to threaten the very workable and practical arrangement they had managed to agree upon.

"'Scuse me…" It was Silas again. She was standing in his way.

"Sorry." She stepped aside. Silas came in, arms full of baby things, followed by Marcus, who carried Ben's suitcases. Preston went out.

Belle focused her mind on putting baby clothes in bureau drawers, a much more productive endeavor than fantasizing about coaxing more kisses from a man she never should have kissed in the first place.

* * *

Within a half hour, she had Ben's things put away. Charlotte brought him in and they put him down for a nap. He went right to sleep, the little angel, even in the unaccustomed room. He was probably exhausted from all the activity and excitement of the morning. There had been way too many changes in his life recently. A child needed continuity. And he would have that. He would have a good life, with his newfound father.

Belle would personally see to it.

There was a small room downstairs off the kitchen. It had a tiny bath with shower. Preston gave that room to Marcus. Charlotte retired to her room across the upstairs hall and Belle went to claim the room next door to Ben's. She had her things put away in no time and then she spent a few minutes working on her list of improvements for Ben's room. Tomorrow, she would drive into town and see what she could purchase there. Then on Thursday, she would go to Missoula, if necessary, to get whatever she hadn't been able to buy in Elk Creek.

Downstairs, she found Charlotte in the kitchen with the housekeeper, Doris, a substantial woman with a broad face and a helmet of steel-gray hair.

"Your Highness." Doris, busy cutting up vegetables at the counter by the sink, gave her a solemn nod of greeting. "I hope you're settling all right."

"I am settling in perfectly. Thank you, Doris—and please, I prefer to be called Belle."

"It don't hardly seem proper," Doris argued. "Bad enough you been upstairs workin' like the hired help." Doris had offered to put Belle's things away for her. Belle had thanked her but said she had no problem taking care of all that herself.

"I'm used to being self-sufficient," Belle told her.

Doris sniffed. "Well, all right, then. And I guess, if that's how you want it, I'll be callin' you Belle."

"I would appreciate that. Thank you."

"We're accustomed to taking care of ourselves," Charlotte said proudly. She sat at the table, sipping coffee and nibbling on what looked like lemon coffee cake. "Belle's work takes her to places where the accommodations can be quite primitive. We manage. It's lovely to be guests in such a clean, well-cared-for home."

Doris gave her a look. "Charlotte, are you butterin' me up?"

Charlotte smoothed her pale brown hair, which she always wore neatly pulled back in a chignon. "It is possible that I am, yes."

Doris blinked and then she and Charlotte laughed together. Belle got herself a cup of coffee, which Doris let her do without a word of protest. Then the housekeeper explained that the McCade men were out with the horses. "They'll be in for dinner, which is pot roast. I take the food over to the men in the cabin and leave it in the oven there, ready for them. I leave everything ready here, too, for Silas and Preston. They usually eat right here in the kitchen. But with you two and the little one and the bodyguard staying for a time, I've gone ahead and set the table in the dining room. You need me, I can stay to serve tonight. I'll just give my Enoch a call and tell him I'll be late."

Belle said, "The pot roast smells wonderful and we can manage just fine."

Doris frowned. "You sure?"

Charlotte chimed in. "You go home to your husband."

"Well, all right, then." Doris told them they were not under any circumstances to clear the table. "I got Silas and Pres trained to put the leftovers away so's they don't spoil. Everything else, I'll take care of in the morning."

"All right, then," said Belle.

"Silas has told me the news," Doris confided. "About that darling boy bein' Preston's. About you bringing him here to his daddy. About his mother's passing. I was very sorry to hear about that, about your loss." She shook her head and clucked her tongue. "I never met her, but I understand she was your friend. It's a sad thing to lose a friend. Especially one who should've had all her life ahead of her. And so hard on the little boy, too."

"Yes," Belle replied, wondering if it would ever get easier to speak about Anne. "Hard on everyone. Thank you, Doris."

Doris clucked her tongue some more and then set to work chopping carrots with gusto. "Preston's a good man," she said. "I think he will be a fine father."

"As do we," Charlotte agreed.

Pres came in at a little after five. He left his dirty boots outside and headed straight up the stairs in his stocking feet to wash off the smell of horse and manure.

The door to the kid's room was wide open. He glanced in there on his way past and saw Belle sitting on the braided rug by the window. She had Ben in her arms and was reading him a picture book.

They looked good together, Belle and the boy. Content. Relaxed. He felt a little jab of guilt, that he would take the child from her.

But it couldn't be helped. The boy was his and belonged with him.

Belle read, "The truck goes *vroom, vroom, vroom.*"

Ben imitated the sound by making a growling noise in his throat. Then he laughed in delight at his own approximation of the noise.

"Very good," said Belle, and kissed the top of his blond head.

That was when the boy glanced Pres's way. He actually tried on a shy little smile. "Hi," he said.

Pres felt a definite tightness in his chest. "Hi."

Belle glanced his way, too. Was that gladness he saw in her eyes at the sight of him?

Oh, come on. Why should she be glad to see him? She was a princess and he was no prince. In a month or so, she'd be outta there. She'd go back to her own world where the men wore designer duds and never smelled like manure.

"Dinner in half an hour?" she asked. "I know it's kind of early, but I thought it would be nice if Ben could eat with us. He gets hungry early."

"Hawngry," echoed Ben. "Hawngry, hawngry. *Vroom, vroom...*"

"Five-thirty's fine," he said. "We always eat around then anyway. Dad should be over from his place in a few minutes. I'm just going to clean up a little."

"Doris said she thought there was a high chair up in the attic?"

He nodded. "Soon's I wash off the grime, I'll go up and get it."

When he emerged from his room ten minutes later, she was waiting for him in the hallway. "I left Ben with the others downstairs. I thought maybe I could help."

It was a job he could have easily managed on his own. But still, it was nice of her to offer a hand. "I warn you, it's dusty up there."

"A little dust is not going to hurt me." She wore gray wool pants and a tan sweater and a pair of low-heeled dark boots and she had her hair swept up, a few curls loose along her cheeks.

He wanted to reach out, catch one of those curls, rub it

between his fingers, to bend close and breathe in the tempting, heady scent of her. But he only shrugged. "All right, then. This way…"

The attic door was near the back stairs. He pulled the chain to lower it and extended the stairs to the floor. He went up, with her behind him. At the top, the light string dangled from the rafters. He gave it a tug.

Bare bulbs glowed along the roofline. He stepped clear of the ladder. She climbed the rest of the way up and then followed him as he made his way, half-crouched, to where the stuff of his childhood was stacked. He pulled off one tarp and then the other, revealing old toys and a couple of trunks and a few pieces of furniture, including the wooden high chair with the back carved with teddy bears twined in ivy. The tray was also of wood. It lifted on a simple hinge.

"A rocking horse," she marveled, touching the big toy's white head, the curling golden mane. She set it to rocking. "It's a beauty. I haven't seen one of these in years and years."

"Paint's a little faded, worn in spots…"

"Was it yours?"

"And my dad's before me. And I believe my grandfather's before him. I think some long-lost great-great-uncle made it. A carpenter, I think he was."

"Oh, and look. A rocking chair…" She rocked it as she had the horse. It creaked just a little. It was plain, of dark wood. He didn't remember it. Had his mother used it when he was a baby?

He had no idea. "Don't tell me. You want me to bring both of them down, along with the high chair."

Her eyes gleamed at him through the dusty dimness. "The rocker, right away, yes. It's nice to have one, especially for reading to him before bed. The rocking motion helps put him to sleep."

"I'll bet."

"They grow so fast. Soon, he'll be too old for rocking to sleep…." Her voice trailed off on an echo of sadness. And then she seemed to shake herself. She said brightly, "And you must promise me that you'll bring the horse down for him when he's a little older."

He was doubtful. "Do kids even care about rocking horses these days? Don't they have Nintendos and iPads and all those other electronic toys to keep them busy?"

"Yes. And electronic devices are wonderful, but so is a rocking horse. Especially a fine one with a golden mane and a gilt-edged red saddle and flaring nostrils like this fellow."

God, she was beautiful. It wasn't fair, wasn't right. How beautiful she was…

"Preston." She said his name so softly.

He remembered to breathe again. "Yeah?"

She only looked at him as he stared back at her. For a long time. Too long, really. They both knew it, as they stood there between the rocking horse and the high chair, in the light of the bare bulb a few feet away.

He never should have kissed her last night. He realized that now. If he hadn't kissed her, he wouldn't know what he was missing. It was probably not a good idea for any man to get a taste of paradise. What man could live with just a taste?

She glanced away. He wanted to reach out, turn her face to him again, pull her close, cover that soft, fine mouth with his.

But he didn't. He resolutely kept his yearning arms at his sides.

And at last, she looked at him again. Now that golden

gaze was careful—and a little too bright. "Well, shall we carry the high chair down?"

"You go ahead. I can manage it."

Belle wasn't surprised when Ben grew fussy during dinner.

It had been a hectic day. And his world just kept on changing. His life hadn't really been what anyone would call normal for months now. He needed consistency and routine. He needed them badly.

When he started throwing cooked carrots, she realized the meal was through.

"Excuse me," she said. "I think it's time for a bath...."

"No!" exclaimed Ben. "No, no, no!" He threw another carrot. It hit Marcus on the cheek. Belle rose then and quickly wiped his hands, as he fussed and wiggled and made his displeasure known.

"I'll take him," Charlotte volunteered.

"Thanks," Belle said. "Don't get up. I've got him."

"He's a feisty one," said Silas, with what actually sounded like approval. "We McCades are a feisty bunch."

"Oh, are you, indeed?" Charlotte asked Preston's father in a tone that could only be called flirtatious.

Silas gave her a look. A very warm, appreciative look. "Yes, ma'am. We most certainly are."

Charlotte and Silas? Surely not...

Ben wailed as she scooped him up out of the chair. "No. Belle, no! No, no, no!"

She left the dining room in a hurry, Ben flailing in her arms.

Upstairs, she took him to his crib and put him into it.

"No. No, Belle, no, no..." He cried and shook his head and waved his little fists.

"I am sorry you are so upset."

"No, no, no, no, no!"

"I am going to leave the room now, Benjamin."

"No! No, no, no no…"

"I will return when you are quiet."

"No, no, no, no!"

Resolutely, she turned and left the room, his wails and "no"s ringing in her ears. With a sigh, she shut the door and sagged against it. His cries were muted now, but no less hard to bear. She knew that such behavior was not the least out of the ordinary for an almost-two-year-old. But still, it wasn't easy to let him cry it out, especially given that he'd lost his mom such a short time ago.

"Could you maybe use a little support?" *Preston.* He stood down the hallway, at the head of the stairs.

She blew out a slow breath and smoothed the front of her sweater where Ben had gripped it in his angry fist. "Support is most welcome. There's nothing as exhausting as a tired, frustrated toddler."

His mouth had a wry twist to it. "I think I'm going to need a nanny."

"Yes." She straightened from the door and went to join him. "I'm sure you will. You can't run a horse ranch *and* be with Ben all day."

He dropped down to sit on the top step. "But not right away. I want him to…know me, to come to trust me first, before he gets attached to a nanny." He patted the empty space at his side.

"That makes complete sense to me." She sat next to him, her ears tuned to the sounds behind the closed door, her mind on those moments in the attic, when she had yearned only to kiss the man beside her a second time. "You'll need to hire someone by the time I leave, though.…" He wore a blue shirt that matched his eyes and he smelled of soap and some bracing, clean-scented aftershave.

"Yeah," he said quietly. "I get that. Will do."

From behind the door, the nos were becoming less frequent, the wailing distinctly diminished. She tipped her head, listening. "He'll be ready for his bath in just a few minutes."

"Is he…is he all right? I mean, Dad said not to get my long johns in a twist over a little temper tantrum. But is that all it is? It can't be easy for him, losing his mom, his whole life turned upside down…"

"He *is* all right," she promised. "Your father's advice is sound. But yes, it doesn't hurt to be extra aware of Ben's moods now, to be sure all his needs are addressed. Losing one's mother is terribly painful and difficult at any age."

He made a noise in the affirmative. "Yeah."

"But you know that," she said softly.

He stared out over the foyer. "It was a long time ago, when my mom died. I hardly remember her. But I do kind of remember that it was bad, that there was…an empty place. A big one that used to be filled up with love and…I don't know, smiles and kisses and cookies and all that stuff."

She studied his profile. He was easy to look at. "What a beautiful way to put it."

He grunted. "I'm just glad—that he's okay, I mean."

"He is. He will be."

"And I want him to start getting used to me being around."

"Yes, he must come to know you, to trust you, to look to you for comfort, to count on you. That's important."

"So I can help with the bath?" He looked so handsome and hopeful. "Or at least, you know, be there, if it doesn't upset him to have me there.…"

"Yes. Absolutely, you may."

"Whew." He braced his arms on his bent knees. "I was

worried you would say no with him already so upset and all."

"Anything that brings you and Ben closer together, nearer to being the family you need to be...I will always say yes to that, Preston." He looked at her then, admiration in his eyes. She wished he would never look away, even though she knew her wish was completely selfish. And purely futile. What could they have together? He loved this ranch. It was in his blood, his DNA.

He wasn't going to leave it to marry a princess and live in Montedoro.

And she believed in the work she did. She found meaning and purpose in her life. Moving to Montana to be a rancher's wife, it wasn't the life she'd always imagined for herself.

So what would they have, then?

A love affair? A fling? She'd never been a woman who engaged in affairs. She didn't think she was ready to become such a woman now.

No, it wasn't going to happen with them.

And she needed to remember that.

She said, "We must speak about Christmas."

"Must we?" He was teasing her.

She remained serious. "Yes. How do you celebrate the holidays here in Montana?"

"In Elk Creek? Enthusiastically. There are any number of Christmassy goings-on. Community events. Church stuff. Here at the ranch? It's been years since we even put up a tree."

"That will have to change. Children need...ritual. They need to celebrate, to experience...wonder. To know joy."

"Joy, huh?" He nudged her with his shoulder, the way he had done that morning, when he finally stopped being so angry about Anne having kept Ben from him.

"Yes," she said firmly. "Joy. Definitely. And you mentioned church activities. What church do you attend?"

"Er, we used to be Catholics, when my mom was alive. Now I would call us basically lapsed."

"Community, Preston. It's so important. And regular church attendance helps a child to feel more a part of his community, to *be* more a part of his community. Plus, it never hurts to bring a child up with an awareness of a higher power."

He was watching her again, his head tipped to the side. "A higher power, huh?"

She nodded. "I'm trying very hard not to be pushy about this."

"But you want me and Dad and Ben to be churchgoing folk."

"At least consider it. We could all go together this Sunday."

"You say that so sweet and all. But I've noticed you're a very strong-minded kind of woman. When you want something done, it tends to get done."

Why lie about it? "I am strong-minded, yes." She gave him a bright smile. "So, then. Sunday Mass. We're agreed on that."

He held her gaze for longer than he should have—longer than she should have allowed. Yearning rose within her for…more. With him. *Of* him. Slowly, he nodded. "Church on Sunday. Sure." He looked out over the foyer again.

With difficulty, she found her voice and suggested, "And as far as the Christmas traditions you need to start establishing, do you have decorations or will we be buying those?"

He answered rather gruffly. "I think we do have decorations up there in the attic somewhere."

"Will you find them and bring them down?"

"I'll do that."

"Wonderful. And we'll need a tree."

"No problem. We got trees coming out our ears around here. We'll find a nice one and cut it down."

She got her legs under her. They were strangely shaky. Holding the banister for support, she rose to her feet. "Hear that?" He gazed up at her. What she saw in those summer-sky eyes of his made her knees go weak all over again. "Silence. Sweet, sweet silence. I do believe that Ben is ready for his bath."

He rose. And then he just stood there, gazing down at her as she gazed up at him.

She wanted to reach for him, to pull that dark gold head down, until his lips touched hers, to thread her fingers in his hair. She *yearned* to reach for him. That yearning rose, like a tide. It spilled upward, overflowing the boundaries of her heart.

He asked, so gently, "Belle?"

She didn't answer. *Couldn't* answer. Resolutely, she turned and led the way back to Ben's room.

Chapter Six

When Belle opened the door, Pres looked in and saw Ben sitting quietly in his crib.

Belle asked, "Are you ready for your bath now?"

The kid seemed to actually consider the question. And then he nodded. "Bath. Yes."

So she went on into the room, scooped him out of the crib and took him to the bathroom, where she filled the tub, helped him out of his clothes and into the warm water.

Ben was subdued. Almost as though he felt guilty for being such a pill. More likely, though, he was just plain exhausted after a hectic day. Plus, he'd expended some serious energy having that tantrum. That had probably worn him out, too. He sat in the tub and yawned and half-heartedly poked at a couple of floaty toys Belle had put in there for him.

The blue-tiled bathroom was good-size, with both a

shower stall and a tub. Plenty of room for Pres to hang out near the door, out of the way.

Belle knelt on the bath mat, soaped up a cloth and washed Ben's face. She sudsed up his little body. Pres watched her, thinking how much he liked her brown hair with its streaks of red and gold. He liked the way she held her back so straight and proud, even on her knees beside a bathtub.

He'd wanted to kiss her, back there at the top of the stairs.

He'd wanted it bad.

And he would have done it if she'd given him the slightest encouragement. He knew she was right not to, but that didn't make him want to kiss her any less.

Ben yawned again. He slumped his soapy shoulders and let out a long sigh. Then he frowned and all at once, he seemed to be seeing Pres. *Really* seeing him, standing there by the door. "Hi," he said, suddenly bright and alert. "Hi."

"Hey, there, Benjamin. How are you doin'?"

Was that too many words? Ben looked at him kind of puzzled. And then, finally, he said, "Hi," again.

"That's your daddy," Belle told him, simple and direct and straight-ahead as you please. Pres's heart ached—a good ache—and his throat felt tight. She dribbled water over those fat little shoulders, rinsing off the soap bubbles. "Can you say that? Say, 'Hi, Daddy.'"

Ben looked at her and laughed. "Belle." He put his little hand over her mouth. "Belle…"

She kissed his fingers. "Say, 'Hi, Daddy.'"

Ben laughed again. And then he got serious. He looked directly at Pres and said, "Hi, Da-da."

Now, there was a moment worth waiting half a lifetime for, a moment a man holds in his heart for all of his days. "Ben," he replied, his voice only cracking a little bit. "Hi."

* * *

The next day, Wednesday, Silas and Preston had work that couldn't wait. They were up and gone before Belle and Charlotte brought Ben downstairs.

Preston had left Belle a note under a magnet on the refrigerator.

"Here," said Charlotte. "Let me have that handsome boy."

"Shar-Shar…" Ben reached for her.

Belle handed him over and took the note off the refrigerator.

Charlotte put Ben in the high chair. She sent Belle a questioning glance. "Anything important?"

"Preston says he and Silas will be back in by early afternoon. And if we go into town this morning, could we stop at Colson's Feed and Seed and pick up an order that should be waiting there."

Charlotte filled Ben's sippy cup and gave it to him. Then she grabbed an apple from the fruit bowl. She got a paring knife from a drawer. Already, she seemed to know her way around the McCade kitchen. "Shopping, hmm? What do you think? I know you have plans for Ben's room."

"Yes," Belle agreed, holding the note that Preston had written, trying not to imagine what it might be like, to get notes like that from him all the time, to have a day-to-day life with a good man like him—and Charlotte was watching her, a funny, knowing look in her eyes. Belle quickly folded up the note and stuck it in her pocket. "We, ah, might as well get started. Ben's room is not going to paint itself." She went to the coffeepot, which was half-full, and poured herself a cup. "Also, I spoke to Preston about church. We'll all be going on Sunday. They're of the Catholic faith." Both she and Charlotte had been raised Catholic.

"Lovely," said Charlotte.

"And as for the holidays, Preston has said there are decorations in the attic, which he will bring down. And they have plenty of trees to choose from right here at the ranch."

"You have it all in order, I see," Charlotte remarked as she set apple slices on Ben's high chair tray. "I do like him," she added in a thoughtful tone. "He's honest and kind. And very handsome, your Preston."

Belle stiffened. "Charlotte, he's not *mine*. Not in any way."

Charlotte wore the most innocent expression. "Excuse me, dearest. I don't know what I was thinking. Of course, he's not *yours*."

Belle felt ridiculously defensive—which was probably why she asked, "And by the way, is there something going on between you and Silas?"

Charlotte chuckled. It was a very knowing chuckle, an almost *sensual* chuckle, which meant it was a completely un-Charlottelike chuckle. Charlotte, after all, had spent her life eradicating all things daring, bold, sensual and dangerous from her personality. She came from a disgraced branch of Belle's mother's family. Charlotte's father had been French, a penniless count, a complete wastrel, and her mother an American showgirl known to have had tempestuous affairs with any number of notorious playboys before marrying the count. Poor Charlotte had spent her life living on the fringes of the aristocracy, working as a governess and companion. She was forever upright and serious in an ongoing effort to live down her parents' awful reputations.

But she didn't seem so very serious now. "What could possibly be going on between Silas McCade and me?" she asked in a voice that came across as both teasing and a little bit naughty.

"Charlotte, what's got into you?"

"I'm sure I have no idea what you're talking about, dear."

"Well, last night, you seemed downright flirtatious with him."

"Was I?" She sliced a banana onto Ben's tray.

"Yum," he said, "'nana…" And shoved a slice into his mouth.

"Yes," Belle said strongly. "And now, well, Charlotte, I think you are teasing me."

"I? Teasing you?" Her cheeks were pink. And her slight smile was completely charming.

Belle knew for a certainty then. There *was* something going on between Charlotte and Ben's grandfather.

And really, was there anything the least wrong with that? Not that Belle could see. If Charlotte was finding a little romance in her life at last, Belle couldn't find it in her heart to be anything but happy for her.

She gave her dear friend an approving nod. "Well, whatever you're *not* doing with Silas, enjoy every moment of it."

"I assure you, I shall."

Doris came in a few minutes later. Marcus joined them. The housekeeper whipped them all up a quick breakfast of blueberry griddle cakes and eggs. When she learned they were driving into town, she had a few staples she wanted them to pick up.

At a little after nine, with Marcus behind the wheel of the SUV, Belle, Charlotte and Ben went into town.

They stopped at Colson's Feed and Seed first. The narrow-eyed strawberry-blonde behind the counter had the animal supplements Preston had ordered.

She was also completely lacking in tact or discretion. "Your Highness," she said with a gap-toothed smile. "I am Betsy Colson and I hear you moved out to Pres McCade's ranch and that Pres is that little boy's daddy."

Before she could answer, Ben, in Charlotte's arms, chortled in delight. "Dada, Dada. Hi, Dada…."

Belle granted the woman a regal nod. "Information certainly flows freely in Elk Creek."

"Yes, it does," Betsy Colson agreed. "I have known Pres McCade since he was knee-high to a bug's butt. And it's kind of a surprise, is all. One minute he's about to marry Lucy Saunders. Then Lucy dumps him for Monty Polk— now what Lucy could have been thinking to dump Pres for Monty…well, I'm not even going to dignify that with wonderin' about it. But after Lucy leaves him at the altar, so to speak, Pres acts like he'll never have anything to do with a woman again. But somehow, all these months later, here comes a real, live princess, a princess with a little boy who looks a whole lot like Pres."

Lucy, Belle thought. Preston had mentioned a fiancée who broke it off with him, hadn't he? That must be Lucy.

And apparently, Betsy Colson was assuming that Ben was Belle's child. Belle considered disabusing her.

But Charlotte caught her eye and gave her the slightest negative shake of her neatly coifed head.

Belle took the hint. Charlotte was absolutely right. There was little to be gained by denying that Ben was hers. And if she did deny it, what next? Was she going to stand there in the feed store and explain to this stranger how Preston and her dear, deceased friend Anne had spent a drunken night together a few Septembers ago and Ben was the result?

Absolutely not. "Betsy, how much do we owe you?"

"Not a thing. It's on Pres's tab—so tell me, when did you first meet Pres? Everyone in town would really love to know."

"I first met Preston on Monday morning in the Sweet Stop Diner."

Betsy frowned. "*This* Monday morning?"

"Yes." Belle picked up the package Betsy had plunked on the counter. "And thank you. Have a wonderful day."

Before Betsy could frame her next question, Belle turned for the door, Charlotte and Ben right behind her. Marcus pulled the door open just as she reached it.

They went to the local paint store next and bought yellow, blue and green paint for Ben's room, along with all the equipment necessary to do the job. There was a bulletin board at the store where local house painters posted their phone numbers. Belle took down three numbers. She also found a Winnie-the-Pooh mural kit. She and Charlotte agreed that Pooh would be good for Ben's room for the next three or four years. Then he would probably insist on changing it. For now, though, Christopher Robin and friends seemed quite appropriate.

Finally, they stopped in at the grocery store and bought the items on Doris's list. They were back at the ranch for lunch, where Doris told them which of the painters whose numbers Belle had collected would do the best job.

Belle called Doris's man. He promised to be there at eight Thursday morning.

Preston came in at two, went right up and had his shower. Belle was waiting for him at the foot of the stairs when he came down.

He stopped in the middle of the staircase, his hand on the railing, and gazed down at her. To her, he seemed pure American cowboy in clean jeans, a belt with a whole lot of buckle, rawhide boots and a heavy corduroy shirt the color of coffee with extra cream. He said, "I met you, what, two days ago?"

Had it been only two days? "That's right."

"So why is it I already know that look in your eye?"

Her eyelashes seemed to be fluttering of their own accord. "What look?"

"That 'I have plans for you' look."

She waved her list of things to do. "Well, yes. There are a few little things...."

"Oh, I'll just bet." But at least his eyes were gleaming and his only slightly swollen mouth *almost* smiled. "I took a peek into Ben's room just now."

"And?"

"Sound asleep."

She nodded. "It was a busy morning. He went right down when I put him to bed after lunch. I wouldn't be surprised if he slept for another hour."

He descended the rest of the way and stopped on the bottom stair. "Dad should be over from his house in a minute." His voice was rough and soft, both at once. So strange, how they could speak of the most mundane things and yet, beneath the ordinary words, so much more was going on. "We'll call a powwow in the kitchen."

"A powwow..." She sounded breathless, which was a little bit ridiculous. A person didn't get out of breath just standing at the foot of the stairs waiting for a certain man to come down.

"Yeah, a powwow. You, me, Dad, Charlotte. We'll take on that list of yours and wrestle it into submission."

Five minutes later, all four of them sat around the table, sipping coffee, enjoying a plate of Doris's chocolate chip cookies fresh from the oven, discussing what needed to be done. Marcus was there, too. He accepted a cookie and then did what he always did—stood quiet and watchful, out of the way.

"A little late in the day for a drive to Missoula," said Silas. "It'll be dark before you know it. Plus, there's snow predicted for later in the evening. You don't want to be stuck out on the highway if the front moves in early."

"All right," Belle agreed. "We'll see how the weather is

tomorrow and if possible, make the drive to Missoula in the morning after I show the painter what I want him to do."

Preston swallowed a bite of cookie. "The painter? Of what?"

"Of Ben's room, remember? I said it needed paint. You agreed that was all right with you...."

"Ah," he said as if maybe he hadn't, but he didn't feel like arguing the point.

She was starting to feel that she'd presumed a bit. So she explained further. "We bought yellow, blue and green paint."

Preston considered that information and then remarked, "That's a lot of colors."

"Children like a bright room. And I promise, the colors go well together. They're not too loud or jarring."

"Whew," interjected Silas, smoothing his mustache and then pretending to wipe sweat from his brow.

Belle added, "I thought one color for each wall...."

Preston grunted. "Whatever you say—and at last count, there were four walls in Ben's room."

"Well, yes. And there will be a mural. We bought a kit for it."

"A mural of what exactly?" He didn't look upset or anything. But he didn't exactly look excited at the idea either.

"It's, um, Winnie-the-Pooh sitting under a tree with a jar of honey and bees buzzing around him. There's Christopher Robin and Eeyore in the background."

Preston sipped coffee. "I'm guessing he'll outgrow that in a flash."

"He's not even two. He won't outgrow Winnie-the-Pooh for years yet."

"You couldn't have picked dinosaurs or horses or trucks or something?"

She felt a sizzle of annoyance with him. "What have you got against Winnie-the-Pooh?"

"I've got nothing against Winnie-the-Pooh. I just prefer horses. Or trains."

Silas chuckled. Belle shot him a quelling glance. The older man put up both hands. "Hey, no problem. Leave me out of it."

Belle glanced at Charlotte for support. Charlotte had her lips pressed together in that way she did when she was trying to be extra dignified but what she really wanted to do was laugh.

Was this little contretemps with Preston humorous, then?

She realized that maybe it was, a bit. She'd decided what she thought was right for Ben. And Preston had his own ideas about that. She was, perhaps, more than a little accustomed to having her own way about such things. Due partly to her background and partly to her high-profile position with Nurses Without Boundaries, people tended to defer to her. She made decisions and choices and she followed through on them, having things her way most of the time. She tried her best to be fair, but she knew she had definite opinions as to how things should be.

However, in this case, she had to remember that the whole idea was to get Preston to feel comfortable taking care of his son. If *he* had strong opinions about what he wanted in his little boy's room, well, that was a good thing, wasn't it?

She knew that it was. But it was also more proof of all the ways she was…losing him.

Losing Ben.

Dear God. Life was cruel. It was her job here, in Montana, to lose Ben. So that Ben could gain his father, so that Preston could have his son.

Sometimes doing what one had to do was too painful for words.

And now it was way too quiet in the kitchen. Neither Silas nor Charlotte looked much like they wanted to laugh anymore.

"Belle…" Preston's voice was gentle.

She swallowed hard, and straightened up in the chair, lifting her head proudly, meeting his beautiful blue gaze. "You're right. I should have considered that you might want to choose something else—or maybe not even have a mural. I could…well, if that's what you want, I…"

"Look, it's all right. Winnie-the-Pooh is fine."

"No," she said. "It's not. We'll choose something else— that is, if you're willing to have a mural in the first place."

"A mural is fine."

"All right, then. Tomorrow, on the way to Missoula, we'll stop in town and trade in Winnie-the-Pooh for trains. Or horses."

"Or cars." He said it lightly. Teasingly.

And she felt better. About everything.

Charlotte said, "Which means, Preston, that you're the one who should go with Belle on the shopping trip tomorrow. That way you'll be there to approve the purchases for Ben's room." She turned to Belle. "I'll keep Ben with me here. It's so much easier to shop without a little one in tow."

Silas said, "Now, that makes sense."

Preston asked him, "Can you handle things on your own tomorrow?"

"I was running this ranch when you were in diapers."

"Okay, Dad. I'll take that as a yes."

So it was agreed. Weather permitting, Belle and Preston would go to Missoula as soon as Belle had put the painter to work the next morning.

The second subject for discussion was Christmas. Specifically, decorating the tree.

Silas said, "We can make this quick. Pres, you go up and bring the decorations down. As I recall, they're just about directly over our heads." He pointed at the ceiling. "You think you can find them? Good. Belle can help you. Right, Belle?"

"Well, ah, certainly."

"And Charlotte and I and the hands will go out and get us a tree. That work for you, Charlotte?"

Was Charlotte actually blushing? "I would love to go and acquire a tree with you, Silas. Are you sure we need both of your hired men?"

"When I say a tree, I mean a *tree*. We'll find us a tall one to stand proud in the front hall—and what are we waiting for?" He shoved his chair back. "Bundle up and let's get a move on."

Ten minutes later, Pres stood under the attic door with Belle. He lowered the ladder and led the way up with Belle right behind him.

At the top, he turned on the attic lights and paused to glance back at her. "This way," he said, all too acutely aware of her, in her trim brown pants that looked pretty amazing coming or going, of that snug sweater she wore that was sort of brown and sort of gold and a little bit amber just like her eyes.

He led the way through the stacks of boxes and crates and old furniture to the place where the old man had said the Christmas things would be. "Here we go." There were boxes and more boxes of varying sizes, stacked close together, each one labeled *Christmas* in his mother's clear, rounded hand.

"There are so many." Belle sounded thrilled.

"Yeah." He felt ridiculously proud of himself, as if he was responsible for all this stuff. He explained, "My mom was really big on Christmas. She always had a twelve-foot tree in the front hall. And then she had miles of garland and lights for outside and in. And a manger scene. And little snow scenes and angels with trumpets. I swear she covered every flat surface in this house with some kind of Christmassy thing or other."

Belle was watching him, her eyes so dark and deep. "You never said how old you were when she died...."

"Nine."

"So sad." She watched him kind of hopefully, like she wanted him to say more.

Why not? "It was a freak riding accident. Her horse got spooked and threw her. She hit her head. Died instantly." He stared at the stacks of boxes. "My dad never had the heart to get all this stuff down again after that."

"Oh, Preston. You haven't had Christmas since you were nine?"

He gave her a shrug and a wry smile to show her it wasn't *that* bad. "Sure, we did. The old man's a good dad. He went out the next year and bought a fake tree and some new decorations. We used those until I was eighteen or so. And then it got seeming a little bit silly, him and me and our fake Christmas tree."

She gazed out over all the boxes and made a small, worried sound. "Will it be hard for you—and your father—to decorate the house with these things of your mother's?"

He shook his head. "Naw. The old man's pretty up front about what he likes and what he doesn't, about what bothers him, in case you haven't noticed."

She chuckled. "You're right. He's quite direct. I *have* noticed."

"If he didn't want us to use all this stuff, he would have said so."

"And you? How do *you* feel about it?"

"Good. It's different now that there's Ben. Ben is…" He paused, seeking the right words. "Ben brings it home, what Christmas is all about. And with you and Charlotte here, it makes the whole thing even more special, you know?"

"Special." She was still watching him. "I'm so glad you feel that way."

All of a sudden, he was kind of embarrassed. He grunted and said gruffly, "I'm only saying it's a good time to haul out all the decorations and do it up right."

"I'm glad." She said it again, so quietly. Like it was a secret. Just between the two of them. The bare bulb overhead cast her face in shadow, put a bronze gleam on her hair.

He thought about her, about her real life. What did he know of the life of a princess? "You won't be home for Christmas this year."

"No, I won't."

"I'll bet your family misses you."

"We're all grown up now. We can't all be together all of the time. But yes, they miss me. And I think of them often."

"You have a tree at the palace in Montedoro?"

She lifted her chin. Those fine eyes gleamed up at him. "Several. Although I don't live at the palace anymore, not since I returned from college here in America. I have my own villa. I travel a lot for my work. When I'm at home, I like having my own place."

"A villa…" He tried to picture her there, surrounded by palm trees, maybe on a terrace, with a view of some exotic, deep blue sea.…

It made him feel rough and uncultured. Beneath her.

She said, "My father…he had a difficult childhood. My grandfather, *his* father, wasn't a nice man."

"The one with the ranch near San Antonio, right?"

"Yes. The ranch called Bravo Ridge. My grandfather, James Bravo, had seven sons. And all but one—the oldest, my uncle Davis—left home by the age of eighteen. They left to get away from Grandfather James, who was both verbally and physically abusive. My grandmother, my father's mother, walked around in a daze most of the time, my father always said. They never really celebrated holidays. And my father always swore that when he had children, things would be different. My mother, the sovereign princess, was in complete accord with him. So in Montedoro, we celebrate every chance we get. At Christmastime, the palace is ablaze with holiday lights. And there are parties and balls. And a candlelight service at midnight on Christmas Eve."

"We have those here—well, not the balls. But we have holiday dances in the Masonic Hall, the Saturday before Christmas, and one on New Year's Eve. And all the churches hold Christmas Eve candlelight services."

A smile played at the corners of her way-too-kissable lips. "And don't forget the Christmas Craft Fair."

He groaned, just to give her a bad time. "That's right. It's this weekend. We can't miss that."

"No, we most definitely cannot." She said it so primly, in the way that Charlotte sometimes spoke. Like a strict schoolteacher or someone on *Masterpiece Theatre*. Kind of stuffy, but in a way that charmed him completely.

Two feet of rough attic floor planks separated them. It seemed much too great a distance. He dared to move closer.

Her eyes widened a little—but she didn't back away. Her scent came to him, sweet and fresh in the dim, dusty space.

And he couldn't resist. The temptation to touch her was too powerful. It burned within him, undeniable.

He gave in to it. He reached out, brushed the back of

his index finger along the velvet curve of her cheek. So smooth. "So beautiful…" It surprised him a little to realize he'd said the last aloud.

She sighed, the sweetest sound. And she whispered, "Really. This is a bit mad, don't you think?"

He'd already gone too far. So he went further still. He stroked his hand down the rich silk of her hair. "Absolutely crazy, I agree."

She tipped her head, the way a cat will do, fitting it more snugly against his stroking hand. "It couldn't…go anywhere."

He admitted, "I know," the two words more breath than sound. And he dared to catch a loose curl, to rub it between his fingers. Not silk after all. Silk couldn't compare.

She reached out then. She put her hand against his chest, over his heart. He was certain she could feel it pounding away so hungrily in there. "Preston…"

"Belle." That did it somehow. The sound of her name on his own lips. It freed him to clasp her shoulder, to pull her closer—all the way. She fit against him as though she was made to be there. "Belle…"

He lowered his mouth and covered hers.

Chapter Seven

Like nothing in the world, nothing he'd ever known before, the taste of her.

He shouldn't want her so much. But he did.

He had wanted her the first second he laid eyes on her, sitting there so serene, so princesslike, in that booth at the diner. It was a wanting that only seemed to increase with every hour, every minute, every beat of his heart.

She made a low, rich, hungry sound and her hand moved upward, to clasp his neck. She wrapped her other arm around him, too. And her lush mouth opened beneath his, inviting him.

He didn't need any more of a welcome. He speared his tongue inside and tasted her fully, his head spinning with the scent of her, his senses on fire with the soft, smooth, perfect shape of her pressed up close against him.

"Mad," she whispered against his mouth.

"Crazy," he agreed, nipping her plump lower lip with his teeth. "We can't..."

"We shouldn't..."

He kissed her some more—deeply. Hungrily. He pulled her up close against him. He was shamelessly hard for her, aching with need in the space of an instant.

She knew. She felt it, too. She pressed her body against him, answering him without words, her slim hips moving, rocking against him, so soft and willing, her body calling to his.

Wrong, his mind chided.

Never so right, his body insisted.

She had hold of his shirt collar, and she was pulling him down to her, her sweet lips open for him, offering him everything, as she kissed him with such heat and intimacy that she blew all rational thought straight to kingdom come.

He was about to scoop her up into his arms and carry her...somewhere. He wasn't sure where.

He couldn't even think straight.

And then, with a low, desperate moan, she let go of his collar. She flattened her hands on his chest—and she broke the straining, starving kiss.

He shook his head, blinked, stared down at her. "Belle. What?" He was panting like he'd just run a long, hard race.

She gazed up at him, eyes wide, the amber lights dominant, hot as molten flame. "Preston." Breathless. Yearning. "Preston, no..."

No.

He shut his eyes. Focused on his breathing, on slowing his galloping heart, on regaining control.

No.

She was right, of course. It was a bad idea.

What he felt for her was dangerous. It could go nowhere. She had her world. This was his.

This time, now, was special. She was here to help him learn to be a dad to Ben. And once that was done, she would go.

That one night with Anne aside—a night he still didn't really remember—he'd never been one to engage in casual affairs. Or any affairs, when you came right down to it.

And really, that was all it could be with her. An affair. Casual. And temporary. A few weeks.

And then over.

He knew himself well enough to realize that if they became lovers, it would be pure hell to learn to live without her. It was probably going to be pretty bad as it was. There was just…something about her.

Something that called to him in a deep way. He'd known her only since Monday and already he understood that she was going to leave a bad emptiness behind when she went, even if he never held her naked body in his arms.

No. He turned the simple word over in his mind. It was a good word, a useful word. Right now, it was the only word.

Carefully, gently, he took her by the shoulders and set her away from him. "You're right. I…understand. We can't be going there. It would only make things tougher in the end."

A hot flush flowed up over cheeks. Embarrassment. "I shouldn't have…I'm sorry, I…"

"Shh." He put the pad of his index finger against her lips—felt the warmth of her sweet breath—and withdrew it. "No apologies. *We* shouldn't have. Let's leave it there."

"But you see, the really bad thing is, I *wanted* to kiss you. So much. It was just like that first night, after the northern lights. It was such a powerful feeling. I couldn't deny it. I didn't *want* to deny it. And it's really not like me. I'm very…practical, really. Very down-to-earth, not prone to flights of romantic fancy."

"Belle, I know."

"And I *still* want to kiss you. Again. And then again after that…"

He tried a smile. It felt too much like a grimace. "You know this isn't helping, right?"

"Oh, Lord." She put her hand against her mouth and stepped back, coming up against a pile of boxes, stumbling a little. He moved to steady her. "Don't…" She put out a hand. "I'm fine." He dropped his arm to his side as she drew herself up tall. "What a mess I'm making of this."

"You're not." He sought the right thing to say, the thing that would reassure her. "It was a kiss. Only a kiss."

Her eyes were huge and haunted. They gave the lie to his denials. But her mouth tried to smile. "Yes, of course. You're absolutely right. Only a kiss…"

And then, from the small baby monitor in her pocket and more faintly from the floor beneath, he heard a fussy little cry. They both stood stock-still, listening.

Saved by the baby, he thought.

The crying continued, grew louder, more insistent.

"You go and take care of him," Pres said. "I'll see about getting these boxes down the stairs."

"Ask Marcus to help you."

"I'll do that. Now go."

With Ben in her arms, Belle stood watching in the archway to the front room as Preston pulled on his sheepskin jacket. It was after six, full dark and snowing. With Marcus's help, Preston had carried all the Christmas boxes down to the foyer. The tree stand waited in the curve at the foot of the stairs.

Outside, Silas, Charlotte and the two ranch hands had returned. Shoving his hat on his head, Preston went out to help them bring in the tree. Marcus put on his coat and followed.

Belle took Ben to the picture window and watched them untie the giant tree from the bed of the pickup. They'd wrapped it in rope, compressing the branches close to the trunk. Belle guessed it had to be at least fifteen feet high. It was going to be quite a project to decorate that monster. They would need a ladder for the side away from the stairs. The good news was that judging by the number of boxes Preston and the bodyguard had hauled down from the attic, they had the decorations to do it.

Charlotte, in her heavy wool coat and a warm wool hat, stood out of the way. Belle couldn't hear what her cousin said, but it appeared that she was giving orders as to how the men should proceed. She waved her mittened hands and clapped and jumped up and down like an excited child. She even threw back her head and laughed once or twice. Belle thought she had never seen her dear friend looking so happy.

Or so free.

Belle could almost envy the older woman. For once, Charlotte seemed willing to simply go where her heart led her, not to worry about the future, about what would happen in the end. Belle wished she could do the same, just surrender to the moment, let her attraction to Preston take her wherever it might.

But that seemed foolish. And somehow wrong. She wasn't here to find romance. She was here to do her duty to her lost friend. She was here for Ben's sake. And for the sake of Preston, too, because he was Ben's father. Getting too close to Preston could make things difficult in the end.

When she signed away her guardianship of Ben, she still hoped to keep her connection with the child, to come and visit now and then, someday even to have Ben visit her in

Montedoro. That might be difficult if she and Preston got involved and it ended badly.

But then she remembered those moments in the attic earlier, and out beneath the stars, after the aurora borealis that first night. When he kissed her, she forgot all the things that mattered most. Duty, responsibility and doing the right thing? All that flew right out the window. She only wanted to keep his strong arms wrapped around her, to feel his mouth against hers, to breathe in the scent of him, to get lost in magic of his tender touch.

"Belle." Ben caught her face between his two little hands and brought her back to the real world. "Belle?" He kept talking, chattering away at her. She didn't understand a word. But she did get that he had realized she'd gone daydreaming and he wanted her back there in front of the window with him.

She kissed his fat, sweet cheek. "Look, Ben." She pointed out the window. "Your daddy, your grandpa and Shar-Shar are bringing in our Christmas tree."

Ben let out another string of nonsense words, smiled broadly and pointed at the group around the bed of the pickup and the long, green, compressed shape of the big tree. "Shar-Shar, Dada, Pawpaw…"

"That's right." She kissed him again. "They'll be bringing that tree in any minute now."

As it turned out, it took a lot longer than a minute. But a half hour or so later, Charlotte held the door open and they brought the gorgeous thing in, stump first. Even tied up, it barely fit through the extra-wide front doorway. With all five of the men helping, they managed to get it upright in the giant tree stand. Then the two hands and Marcus and Preston held it in place while Silas and Charlotte got down on the floor and turned the enormous screws to hold it upright. Belle's task was to tell them when they had it straight and to make sure it stayed that way as Charlotte and Preston's father adjusted the screws.

Ben squirmed to get down, but Belle kept him in her arms. She could see that it was going to be a challenge, keeping an eye on Ben when he was near the tree. He was already walking and he would be pulling on the branches and grabbing for the ornaments every chance he got. But he would learn. Somehow, all children did.

She sighed in delight as the men unwound the rope and the thick branches opened wide in all their fragrant evergreen glory.

Charlotte, who had come to stand beside her by then, sighed, too. "Oh, I do love the scent of a fresh-cut tree."

Silas, who was rolling the rope back up, remarked, "We got ourselves a real beauty, I think." He was looking at Charlotte and his expression said that the tree wasn't the only thing he found beautiful. Watching him, Belle felt tender and protective toward both him and Charlotte. She also felt wistful. And she was very careful not to glance in Preston's direction.

Then Ben exclaimed, "Hawngry! Hawngry!" which made everyone laugh.

Charlotte took charge. "Well, young man, then we shall have dinner."

The ranch hands, a pair of lean, quiet men whose names were Jack and Vince, stayed to eat with them that night. They had Doris's wonderful chicken and dumplings and apple pie for dessert. When Jack and Vince went back across the yard to the cabin, Preston gave them the second pie to share later.

By then, it was time for Ben to get ready for bed. Charlotte and Silas got started putting the lights on the tree. Marcus helped. For a few minutes, Belle stood at the foot of the stairs with Ben in her arms, watching her friend and the elder McCade hauling out the long strings of Christmas lights from a couple of the boxes.

Preston came and stood beside her. A little thrill spiraled through her, just at his nearness.

Ben chortled, "Dada, Dada," and swayed toward him.

Belle shook herself free of the cobwebs of frustrated desire and saw the moment for what it was: a great opportunity. "Here. Carry him up." Preston looked slightly terrified, but he rose to the challenge. He held out his arms and Ben, still giggling, went into them. "All right," she said. "Upstairs we go...." She gestured for Preston to take the lead. Preston started up.

Ben looked over Preston's shoulder, eyes wide and anxious. "Belle?"

"Right here." She started up behind them.

The minute he saw she was following, he relaxed and let the big man called Dada take him up. He held Preston around the neck and babbled away at him, telling him any number of important things in a language only Ben understood.

Upstairs in the big bathroom next to Charlotte's room, Belle took over long enough to stand Ben on a stool at the sink and brush his teeth. He was good that night, putting up with the brushing process, which as a rule he fussed over.

She caught Preston's eye in the mirror over the sink. "You should brush his teeth twice a day, and especially before bedtime. Slowly, you can start showing him how to do it himself."

"How many teeth does he have now anyway?"

"Thirteen. And more coming in all the time. Teething can be painful for him. He'll be fussy and want to chew on a cold teething ring or a biscuit. You can also give him a children's painkiller if a new tooth is really hurting him." She turned to Ben. "Spit."

He did, with enthusiasm.

She filled a glass so he could rinse and spit again. More water ended up on the sink edge than down the drain. She grabbed a towel and blotted it up.

Then she got him under the arms and swung him off the stool. "There we go. Now Dada will help you get out of those clothes."

Belle filled the tub as Preston undressed him. Ben watched Preston solemnly and a little bit warily, but he allowed Preston to guide his arms out of his shirt and lay him gently down on the thick bathroom rug to take off his shoes and socks, his little trousers and his diaper. Belle took him and put him in the tub. He laughed then, and splashed a little, and played with his toys.

Belle washed him. And then she asked Preston to get the towel. She let Preston pull him out of the water and dry him off, after which she picked him up again and carried him to the bedroom changing table, where she put on a fresh diaper and his Cookie Monster pajamas.

"We're going to have to teach Dada to change your diapers," she said to Ben.

Preston, right behind her where she was all too aware of him, said, "It doesn't look all that hard."

"Great. You can do the next one."

"How soon until he learns to use the toilet?"

"Every child is different. I brought along a good book on potty training. It's over there in the bookcase." She snapped the last snap on the blue pajamas. "There. All ready for bed. Would you like a story, Benjamin?"

"Yes!"

"Dada will read to you."

Ben considered that idea, while Preston stood a few feet away trying to look relaxed and willing but not too eager. Finally, Ben commanded, "Dada. Yes."

Belle was tempted to hand Preston the Winnie-the-Pooh picture book just to watch his reaction. But she kept her wickedness in check and chose a story about trucks.

"Dada loves trucks," she told Ben. "And horses and cars. And trains as well."

"Rub it in," Preston said darkly.

Ben stuck his finger in his mouth, sighed and drooled. He was fading fast and would probably go right to sleep if she just put him in his crib, kissed him and said goodnight.

Still, they were doing amazingly well at nudging him toward thinking of Preston as a caregiver. Plus, they *had* promised him a story. She handed Preston the book. "Take the rocker."

Preston settled into the chair he'd brought down from the attic the evening before. She handed Ben over to him.

They made the cutest picture, the big cowboy and the small child in the Cookie Monster pajamas, rocking slowly in the old rocking chair. Preston started reading. Belle edged her way toward the door, thinking she would just go stand in the hall, let it be a moment between Preston and his newfound son—but be ready in case they needed her again.

But Ben stiffened. "Belle. No." He reached out a little hand. Preston looked at her pleadingly.

So she went and sat beside them on the rug. Preston continued with the story of what trucks do at night when no one is watching.

Ben was asleep by page ten. Still, Preston turned the pages and read on to the end. After that, he just sat there, holding the sleeping child, rocking gently, for several minutes more. Belle waited, cross-legged on the floor, not wanting to move and ruin the mood of quiet contentment that seemed to have settled over the room like a cozy, soft blanket.

Finally, Preston whispered, "Look at these hands...." He had one of Ben's hands. The plump little fingers were curled loosely around his index finger. "Amazing."

Quietly, with care, Belle unfolded her legs and rose. "Yes, they are. Amazing."

"I never knew...." With his thumb, he caressed the small hand wrapped around his finger. "I kind of thought all this had somehow passed me by."

"Surprise," she said very softly.

He tipped his head up. In those blue eyes, she saw real wonder. "I had so much to do, goals for the ranch, for my horses. I never had time for meeting a woman, getting to know her, going on dates, all that. Then, a few years back, I decided I was going to have to...get busy or I would never have a family. Lucy...did I mention Lucy?"

"You mentioned a fiancée." And the woman at the feed store had said her name was Lucy.

"Lucy Saunders. That was her maiden name."

Belle gave him a slow nod, standing there above him, thinking she could stand there forever, watching him gently rocking Ben, listening to his low, murmured words.

He said, "Lucy worked at the diner back then. She... flirted with me. One day I just asked her if she wanted to go out to dinner. She said yes. I decided right then that she would be the one. It was a practical decision to me. I'd decided I needed a wife and I wanted to get on with it. I didn't want to waste any time about it."

Belle almost laughed. She put her hand over her mouth. "Oh, Preston. That's terrible."

He put a finger to his lips to warn her not to wake the child. And then he confessed, still whispering, "I know. I mean, I can see that now. And as I already mentioned, it didn't work out. Really got me down when she dumped me. More because it hurt my pride and messed up my plans for a family than anything else—and I can see in those big eyes of yours that you think it was all my fault."

"I didn't say that."

"But you were thinking it—and maybe you're right. But anyway, I decided then that I was no good with women and probably I shouldn't even try."

"Trust me, Preston. You're good with women."

He gazed up at her for a long time. She had a delicious and dangerous sensation of heat and weakness low in her belly. "It's different," he said at last. "With you. You're not like other women."

"Yes, I am."

He shook his head. "You're not like any woman I've ever known. You're special. You're even a princess. We don't get a lot of princesses here in Elk Creek."

"I'm a woman, like any woman." She was watching his mouth, thinking how very simple it would be to bend down, to fit her mouth to his, to share his breath, to taste the slick, hot flesh beyond his lips.

"You ought not to look at me like that, Belle. It's dangerous. For both of us."

She knew he was right. And hadn't they already been through this that very afternoon up in the attic?

So what? I don't care. There's a little slice of heaven here, and I want it. No matter the price...

He had his face tipped up to her, and the look in his eyes said he knew exactly what she had in mind, that he wasn't going to refuse her if she just couldn't help herself....

Oh, she was hopeless. Hopeless and she knew it. She was acting like some lovesick youngster with a first crush. Swearing off kisses in the afternoon, and then ready to fall into his arms just a few hours later. But so what? Her heart and her mind were at odds. Right now, her mind was *not* winning.

One kiss—one *more* kiss. How much could that hurt?

Breathless, yearning, not even caring how silly and contrary she was being, she started to bend down to him.

Ben came to her rescue by stirring, whining a little, shaking his head.

Belle jerked upright again and smoothed her hair, although she hadn't done anything to muss it. Yet. "We should put him to bed...."

"I guess we should." There was humor beneath the words. And a certain roughness that told her he'd wanted to kiss her, too.

Carefully, gathering Ben close, he rose. He carried the sleeping child over to the crib and laid him down in it. Ben didn't stir again. Preston pulled up the blankets and smoothed them over him. And then they tiptoed from the room, turning off the light, but leaving the door open.

Preston took her arm gently and said in that low, quiet voice meant for her ears alone. "Okay. Now I suppose you can kiss me if you really, really want to."

She stifled a laugh. "You are incorrigible."

"I told you. I'm no good with women."

"That's not what I meant."

"Then suppose you tell me what you did mean?"

Oh, she was tempted. But no. "Suppose we just...let it be? Suppose we forget how foolishly I've been behaving, and just go downstairs and help Charlotte and Silas with the tree I insisted you *had* to have?"

He regarded her, suddenly solemn. And then he asked in a neutral tone, "Is that what you really want?"

No, it's not. Not what I really want at all. "Yes, please."

He gestured her ahead of him. "All right, then. Let's go."

The five of them worked on the tree until ten. Then Marcus said good-night. Belle, Charlotte, Preston and

Silas kept at it until after midnight. There were still more Christmas treasures to hang. Preston's mother had collected some beautiful ornaments. And there were acres of fancy red bead garland to put on the tree once all the ornaments were hung. And old-fashioned icicles, too.

Belle hadn't really appreciated what a big job it was, to decorate a home for the holidays. After all, in Montedoro, at the Prince's Palace and at her villa, there were professional decorators and servants who did most of the work. Belle and her family would help out a little, hanging a favorite ornament here and there, but mostly supervising, making certain the end result pleased them.

At the McCade ranch house, they all had to pitch in or the Christmas decorating wouldn't get done. Belle thought that was a good thing. There was satisfaction in the accomplishment, a feeling of ownership, that one had worked hard creating something festive and beautiful for everyone to enjoy.

They agreed they would finish the following night—or at least try to. Charlotte said she would make what progress she could on the tree while looking after Ben the next morning. And tomorrow in the afternoon, if it wasn't too cold out, she and Silas would go to work on the outside lights.

There were still groups of figurines to adorn mantels and tabletops. There were boxes full of garland to string along the staircase banister.

"Little by little," Charlotte said. "It's weeks yet until Christmas."

"Two to be precise," Belle reminded her.

Charlotte laughed in that light, happy way that was so new to her. "We'll do what we can. What we feel like doing. There's no law that says we have to use every beautiful ornament in every one of these boxes."

Belle said good-night and climbed the stairs. In her room, she shut the door and sat on her bed and wished she had kissed Preston more than once in the attic, that she had kissed him in Ben's room that night and in the upstairs hall the night before....

She wished she had kissed him every chance she got, and she knew it was wiser that she hadn't.

Honestly, she needed to get a firm grip on her own emotions. Tomorrow, she would be with him all morning and probably into the afternoon as they shopped for bedding and curtains to brighten up Ben's room. And then they would return to the ranch, where she would see him constantly, where it was her job to take every opportunity to make him and Ben more comfortable with each other.

She had to face it. She was going to be around Preston a whole lot in the coming weeks. She had better decide how to behave and then show a little consistency about it.

Outside in the upper hall, she heard footsteps. Preston. Already, she knew his steady, measured tread. She heard him go into his room and shut the door.

And she longed to get up and go to him. To ask him to please, please kiss her again. To beg him to hold her close in his big arms and tell her all the ways she was different from other women. Tell her that she was special.

And when he'd finished telling her how wonderful she was, he could kiss her some more. He could do a lot more than kiss her....

Belle groaned and buried her face in her hands.

She needed a friend. A confidante. Right now, this very moment. Maybe Charlotte had come upstairs without her hearing. She went to the door and quietly opened it.

Across the hall, Charlotte's door stood wide. Her bed was neatly made. One of her favorite scarves, of lavender-colored wool, lay thrown across the foot of it. No sign of Charlotte. The bathroom door next to her room stood open, too.

From downstairs, faintly, she heard a woman laugh—Charlotte. And then a man's deep chuckle in response—Silas.

So then, Charlotte was still down there with Preston's father, laughing in that new, light, carefree way of hers, no doubt sharing warm, teasing looks with a man she'd met only two mornings before.

And it wasn't that Belle begrudged her dear friend a little romance. She didn't. Not at all. She only wished Charlotte would come upstairs so that Belle could confess to her what a complete idiot she was thinking about being with Preston.

Belle ducked back into her room and shut the door.

Between Montana and Montedoro, there was an eight-hour time difference. That meant it would be almost nine in the morning there.

Would her sister-in-law Lili be up yet? Were Lili and Alex even in Montedoro now?

Belle had always felt she could tell Lili anything. When they were growing up, Lili visited Montedoro often. Lili's mother and Belle's mother had been close friends. Lili was as much a sister to her as her own four sisters, as Anne had been.

She got out her cell phone, but then hesitated to call. Most likely Lili and Alex were in Lili's country, Alagonia, by now. Lili was due to have her twins within the month and she would want her heir to be born in Alagonia.

And the more Belle considered calling Lili, the more certain she became that wherever Lili was right now, she would be with Alex, perhaps having breakfast, or even lingering in bed. Alex had always been the gruff and brooding one in the family. He was much easier to be around now that he had Lili. But still, Belle felt uncomfortable at the idea of discussing her forbidden desire for the rancher down the hall with one of her brothers listening in.

So she called Rhiannon. Rhia, who lived on her own not from the palace, was sixth born of Belle's siblings. Their four brothers were born first. Then Belle, Rhia, Alice, Genny and Rory.

Rhia was an expert on art and antiquities. She worked at the National Museum of Montedoro, advising on acquisitions, overseeing the restoration of the art treasures of centuries.

And she answered the phone on the first ring. "Belle, I'm glad you called. I've been wondering how things are going with Ben, with…everything."

Her sister's voice warmed her, made her feel a little misty-eyed, too. "Oh, Rhia. It's been such a difficult time."

"I don't doubt it."

"I take it you made it home safe and sound." Most of the family had come to Raleigh for Anne's funeral. They'd all known Anne and been fond of her. In the summers during the years they were at Duke together, Anne would often come and stay in Montedoro.

"A smooth, easy trip," Rhia told her. "But a sad one. I still can't believe we lost Anne. It just doesn't seem right, doesn't even seem possible." In her voice was the tightness of held-back tears.

Belle felt her own tears welling in response. "No," she answered a little raggedly. "It doesn't seem possible that she's gone…."

There was a silence, a heavy one. Then Rhia asked, "So how's Ben doing?"

"Remarkably well. We've had a few rough patches. Little tantrums. And when he gets upset, sometimes he calls for her. Slowly, though, I know he'll get over that. Children are so good at living in the present. And that's as it should be...."

"But still." Rhia spoke in a near-whisper. "It's another way we're losing her."

"Exactly. So I try to focus on the good things. Overall, Ben is bearing up beautifully."

"I'm glad." Another silence. Then Rhia said, "I understand you went ahead to Montana to contact the father?"

"Mother told you?"

"Yes. How is that working out?"

Belle brought her sister up to speed on her trip to Montana, on Preston and Silas and all of it so far. She did get a bit sidetracked as she explained in detail what a fine man Preston was. But eventually she caught herself and concluded with, "So right now, I am calling you from the McCade Ranch near the charming small town of Elk Creek."

"You like the father, this Preston McCade. I can hear it in your voice when you speak of him."

"I was that obvious?"

Rhia made a low sound of understanding. "You're attracted to him."

"He's a good man, Rhia. Trustworthy. Strong. Determined. And intelligent, with a sense of humor."

"Does he have a brother?"

Belle laughed. "I'm afraid not."

"Oh, well," Rhia teased. "If I can't have him, I'm happy for you."

"I wish. But you know how it is for us." By *us,* Belle meant herself and Rhia and their sisters, too.

Rhia knew exactly what she was talking about. "I do, yes." Her voice was weary. "The grasping, selfish types can't wait to marry a princess. The good men always think they aren't good *enough.*" Belle's sister spoke from intimate experience. Rhia rarely talked about the man she'd always loved, not even to her sisters—and she never said his name. Belle had no idea who the man was, but she knew the story. He was a commoner and he'd ended their love affair because he felt he was beneath her. Since then, Rhia had been engaged twice, but broken off those relationships before the wedding. "There have to be other men in the world like Father, haven't there?" Rhia tried for lightheartedness, and only fell a little short. "There have to be a few men who are both good *and* willing to give a princess a chance."

"Well, I certainly hope so."

Rhia made a thoughtful sound. "You're saying Preston McCade isn't willing?"

"I don't think he's ready to drop everything and move to Montedoro. And I don't think he would accept the idea of my moving here. "

"Did he say that?"

"Not in so many words, but my feeling is he sees me as…out of his reach."

"You could show him otherwise."

It was just what she'd been longing to hear. "Oh, Rhia. Do you think so?"

"I do. Just because it didn't work out for me doesn't mean it's hopeless for all of us—and besides, why worry now about what will happen in the future? You only just met the man, right?"

"Right. But somehow, it feels as though I've known him forever."

"Isn't that a good thing—that you feel an affinity with him?"

"Yes, of course it is. I can see already that he's going be a good father to Ben. I'm so pleased about that."

"I can imagine that must be a great relief—but also sad

that you won't be bringing Ben home where we can all shower him with love and attention."

Belle felt a bit choked-up again. She managed a low sound of agreement.

And Rhia asked, "How long do you plan to stay there in Montana?"

"Through the holidays at least."

"We'll miss you here.…"

"Miss you, too."

"But, Belle, maybe the best thing is to give it a chance with this rancher of yours."

"He's not mine."

Rhia chuckled. "I knew you would say that."

"Stop teasing me. I mean it."

"All right. But listen, take it from one who knows. Sometimes it's true that things don't work out, but they will never work out if you don't at least try. You'll spend your life wondering what *might* have been if you'd taken a chance. And think about it. You're always so busy running around the world, speaking out for other people. It's important, the work you do. But it's also all-consuming. When's the last time you went out to dinner with an attractive man?"

Belle smiled to herself. "Monday night. With Preston. We went to The Bull's Eye Steakhouse and Casino."

"Sounds…rustic."

"It was. Rustic and charming and so lovely. I had such a fine time with him—at least I did until I finally had to tell him about Ben. Things got difficult then, but we worked through it."

"Belle, I know it's been awful for you these past long weeks, having to be there for Anne at the end."

"I *wanted* to be there."

"Of course you did. But that didn't make it easy or pleasant, having to watch your dearest friend die, arranging her funeral and then finding out she wanted you to handle the job of tracking down Ben's father."

"She couldn't do it, for some reason. But it needed doing. At least she made herself deal with it at the end. She found a way to make it happen."

"Belle, I'm not blaming Anne. Honestly. I loved her, too. I'm only saying that you really do need a little joy in your life. Before the tragedy with Anne, you were working all the time. So now you have a few brief weeks there in Montana, through the holidays, to help Ben and his new-found father make a family together. If it's going well, I'm so glad. And I want you to enjoy every moment."

"Dangerous advice."

"Perhaps."

"Definitely."

"If there's something between you and Preston, why not just go with it, see where it leads you? At the very least, you might end up with a few precious memories to treasure."

"And what about a broken heart? I could also end up with that."

"Yes, you could," Rhia agreed. "But that's always the risk, isn't it, when you take a chance on something important? On the other hand, you could *not* take a chance. You won't get hurt that way. But you'll never find the kind of love that lasts a lifetime either."

Chapter Eight

In the early morning, Belle woke to the sound of Ben fussing in the room next door. She pushed back the covers, pulled on her robe and went to him.

Charlotte, fully dressed in the same clothes she'd worn the day before, was already there and lifting him out of the crib. "It's all right, darling." She sent Belle a glowing smile. "I'll take him down with me."

"Shar-Shar." Ben sighed and leaned his head on Charlotte's shoulder. He waved at Belle in that special way of waving he had—opening and closing his small fist.

She waved back, her heart melting just at the sight of him. "Good morning, my darling."

Charlotte carried him to the changing table, laid him down and unsnapped his pajamas. "Let's get you a fresh diaper first of all, shall we, young man?"

"Yes!"

She hummed under her breath, an old French lullaby,

as she changed him. Belle, leaning sleepily in the doorway, thought that her friend had never looked prettier. Or younger. Or quite so happy.

Charlotte glanced over her shoulder again. "Go on. Have your shower. That painter fellow will be arriving before you know it."

"Right." Belle covered a yawn and turned for the bathroom across the hall. The door to Charlotte's room stood open. Belle glanced in there. The bed was neatly made, the lavender wool scarf tossed across the foot of it, in the same place it had been the night before.

Belle grinned to herself. Had Charlotte slept in that bed last night? Belle's guess was no.

Apparently, Charlotte was the brave one, finally taking a chance on love. Risking her heart. Or maybe just collecting a few precious memories to treasure, as Rhia had suggested Belle ought to do.

Belle thought about her sister's advice several times that day as she and Preston, Marcus in their wake, went from store to store in Missoula, ordering blinds and curtains, buying linens for Ben's bed and a new rug, bright blue with an airplane motif. All the stores were decorated for the holidays. Christmas tunes played everywhere they went. It was quite festive, she thought. They stopped in at a toy store and a kids' clothing store and got a head start on Ben's Christmas gifts, too.

For lunch, they found a little restaurant there in Missoula that served barbecue. Marcus took a seat at the counter, out of the way. And it was almost as if she and Preston were all alone. She gazed at him across the table and thought how she really wasn't up for a holiday fling. She felt more than a little fragile, with the loss of Anne, and with the day drawing near when she would have to say goodbye to Ben.

She did not want to get her heart broken any more than it already was.

But even if she never felt Preston's strong arms around her again, this day was special. Marcus was so skilled at playing invisible that it did feel like it was just the two of them, sharing barbecue and tall, frosty glasses of root beer, talking about their purchases, about whether the snow would hold off long enough for them to get back to the ranch. This simple lunch, this whole wonderfully ordinary day of being together, it all definitely qualified as a memory to treasure.

And she would. She would treasure it. For all of her life.

On the way back, they stopped in at the paint store in Elk Creek. They traded in the Winnie-the-Pooh mural kit for one of a train rolling along a track in a country setting, an airplane flying by in the clouds above. It was snowing as they headed for the ranch. They made it into the yard before it really started coming down thick and heavy.

Inside, there was a large, wonderful-smelling pot of stew on the stove and Doris was just leaving. Preston paid the painter, Richard Gibbons, for his day's work and showed him the mural kit. Richard said he could put it up, no problem. He would be back in the morning to take care of it.

Ben was still napping and Charlotte and Silas were hard at work on the house-decorating project. They had actually finished the tree, which was so beautiful, thick with lights and sparkly ornaments, draped in red bead garland and thousands of silvery icicles. No, they hadn't gotten around to putting up the outside lights yet, but they had arranged cute snow scenes on the mantels in the family room and the front room and put up a manger scene on a long shelf in the foyer. The two looked quite proud of themselves. Charlotte was pink-cheeked and blushing. And Silas couldn't seem to take his eyes off her.

Belle observed the two fondly and more than a little wistfully. But then she asked herself again where it could go with her and Preston anyway?

He was an American, a horse rancher to the core. And she had a rich life, a full life, as a princess of Montedoro, as a spokesperson and fundraiser for causes that needed a strong, determined voice. They had nothing in common but a small boy who had lost his mother.

Or so she was constantly reminding herself.

That night, after Ben was in bed, Marcus retired to his room. The other four adults watched a Western and then a comedy on the big-screen TV in the family room. Belle went up to bed—alone—at a little after eleven. She called her mother in Montedoro just to bring her up to speed on her progress uniting Ben with his father.

Her mother was fond with her, and gentle. She didn't ask a lot of questions. That had never been Her Sovereign Highness's way. But Belle always hung up from a conversation with her feeling loved and accepted and unequivocally supported in any decision she might make, any action she might choose to take.

Friday when Belle got up, the McCade men were already out with the horses and had been for hours. Richard Gibbons arrived at a little after eight and went to work on the mural up in Ben's room. Doris arrived at nine and started making Christmas cookies. Charlotte and Belle pitched in. They even got Ben involved, rolling out a bit of dough for him and helping him press the cookie cutter to make a cookie snowman and a star.

The painter finished the mural at around eleven. Belle thanked him and paid him for the day. Later, after lunch, when Ben went down for his nap, Doris said she'd keep an eye on him. Charlotte, Belle and Marcus got to work putting up the outside lights. They were at it for about an hour when Preston and Silas appeared and pitched in.

Belle went in to get Ben up at a little after three. She bundled him into his warmest clothes and took him outside, where the others were just finishing up. They'd dragged the two tall ladders around the yard, stringing lights on not only the main house, but Silas's place and the hands' cabin as well. They even wound lights up the wide trunk of the giant pine in the center of the driveway.

"We'll be lucky we don't blow all the circuits when we turn all these babies on," Silas warned, looking way too excited at the prospect.

Charlotte chided, "Then perhaps we shouldn't have strung up so many."

Preston laughed and told them all not to worry. He'd had a bigger breaker box put in a couple of years ago and he was sure it could handle the extra load. He also had spare timers from the system he used in the stables, so he hooked up the outdoor lights to come on about dark and go off at midnight.

The lights came on at five. They all went back outside then and stood in the middle of the yard and admired their handiwork.

"Glorious," declared Charlotte.

"Mighty fine," Silas agreed, putting his arm around her.

Charlotte basked in the moment, gazing up at Silas with stars in her eyes. Belle could almost envy the two of them.

They seemed so very happy together.

That night was like the nights before it. Belle and Preston put Ben to bed as a team. Belle went upstairs to her room at around eleven. She heard Preston come up a little while later.

If Charlotte came up after that, Belle didn't hear her.

The next day was Saturday, and that meant the Christmas Craft Fair in town. The McCade men were out working early, but they came in at a little after ten. So did Vince and Jack. They wanted to go into town for the festivities, too.

By eleven, they were on their way, Vince and Jack in Jack's pickup, Marcus in the SUV with Charlotte and Silas in the backseat. Belle, Preston and Ben rode in Preston's four-door truck.

It was a great day, Belle thought. There was more going on than she had realized. The town hall was filled upstairs and down with craft and food booths. There apparently wasn't enough room for all of the booths in that one building. The overflow took up the main floor of the Masonic Hall down at the far end of Main Street.

After they toured the town hall upstairs and down, they went to the diner to grab a late lunch. That took a while. The Sweet Stop was packed that day. But eventually, they all got a booth together—minus Jack and Vince, who had taken off on their own. They had sandwiches and hot chocolate. Ben was adorable and not the least fussy. Belle dared to hope he might last into the evening without getting too worn out. They might even make it to the talent show and bake sale auction that would start at seven in the historic Elk Creek Theater.

Already, Ben was so easy and comfortable with Preston. The little boy spent much of the day in his father's arms, or with Preston pushing his stroller. As they admired handmade Christmas decorations in the Masonic Hall, Betsy Colson from the hardware store appeared.

"Why, Preston," Betsy declared. "That little boy looks exactly like you."

Preston beamed. "So I've been told." And Ben hugged him close and buried his face against Preston's neck the

way he would do with Belle or Charlotte when strangers
had him feeling shy.

The sight had Belle smiling through misty eyes. Already, Ben felt safe with Preston. It had happened so
swiftly—more swiftly and more easily than she had ever
imagined it could. And that meant there would be no need
for her to remain in Montana past the first of the year. All
too soon, her time in Elk Creek would be ending.

"Nice to see you, Your Highness," said Betsy.

Belle put on a big smile. "It's lovely to see you, too,
Betsy."

By six, Ben was fast asleep in his stroller. He'd dropped
off without a peep. People said how adorable he was, sleeping like an angel.

Preston pushed the stroller back up Main, Belle at his
side, Silas and Charlotte right behind them, Marcus taking up the rear.

"Look," said Silas, "they've got the theater doors open."

Preston asked Belle, "What do you think?" He was a fast
learner. He knew already that toddlers lasted only so long
before you had to take them home and tuck them into bed.

"We could go in," she suggested. "If he wakes up and
starts fussing, we'll just have to leave."

"All right, then," he agreed.

She met those blue eyes and she felt downright breathless. He really did have a powerful effect on her senses. One
would think she would grow accustomed to being near him.

But so far, just meeting his eyes, smelling that fresh,
bracing aftershave he wore…it never failed to make her
breath catch and her belly fill with frantic butterflies.

He tipped his hat at an elderly couple as they approached
going the other way.

"Preston," said the white-haired woman. "Silas, hello."

"Mary Beth, John, how're you doing?" asked Silas.

They all paused right there on the sidewalk. Silas made the introductions. The couple's last name was Deluca.

John said, "Delighted to meet you ladies."

Mary Beth declared that Ben was "Quite a handsome child." She also remarked that it had been much too long since she'd seen the McCade men at Sunday Mass.

Preston sent Belle a wry look and replied, "Well, Mary Beth, it just so happens we'll be attending nine o'clock Mass tomorrow morning."

"Excellent," replied Mary Beth. "We will see you there." The Delucas moved on.

There were a lot of people filing in the wide-open double doors of the old theater. And by then, Silas and Marcus had their arms full of purchases. Charlotte and Belle each carried a couple of shopping bags. It seemed pointless to haul everything into the crowded theater with them.

Belle suggested, "Why don't Marcus and I take all the shopping bags to the SUV? We'll meet you inside."

Nobody argued. Silas and Charlotte handed over their purchases and Preston gave her the big bag he'd hooked to the stroller handle.

The SUV was in the lot next to the diner. It didn't take long to stow all the bags in the back.

Belle and Marcus entered the lobby of the Elk Creek Theater only a few minutes after they'd left the others. It was wall-to-wall people inside. Tables lined the walls, covered with red-and-green cloths and all manner of tempting baked goods, each with a little card in front of it that described the item and announced who had baked it. There were pies, cakes, cookies and cupcakes. All of it looked good.

The crowd was noisy, everyone chatting and laughing.

Larry Seabuck from the Drop On Inn appeared at Belle's side. "Ma'am, how are you doing?"

She gave him a careful smile. He tended to fawn over her and it made her uncomfortable. "Hello, Larry. I'm doing quite well, thank you."

He leaned a little too close. "The idea, ma'am, is that everyone gets a good look before the auction starts. Ahem. People decide what they want to win. Men make sure of which pie or cake the wife or the sweetheart made with her own little hands. It gets the competition going when the bidding starts. And more competition means more money for this year's worthy cause—which I see by that big banner on the wall by the door, is the old theater itself this time. Ahem." His wire-rimmed glasses had slipped down his nose. He pushed them back up. "I believe they want to put in a new sound system and replace some of the seating."

"Thank you, Larry," she said, and edged away from him as his wife, RaeNell, stepped up and slipped her arm in his.

"Nice turnout, don't you think, Your Highness?" Rae-Nell slid a narrow-eyed glance from Belle to her husband and back again.

Belle was more than ready to move on. "Very nice. Good to see you, RaeNell." She turned for the next table, murmuring "Excuse me" as she slipped around a young couple holding hands and whispering together. Marcus was right behind her, keeping close the way he always did in crowds.

The lobby wasn't very big and she spotted Preston instantly. He stood across the room, near the wall, looking so tall and solid and manly. He was watching her, waiting for her.

Her heart lifted. For a split second, the space cleared in front of him and she saw the stroller, with Ben in it, still sound asleep, his head drooping to the side, his plump lower lip stuck out and his dimpled chin tucked low into his blankets. Tenderness filled her. For the child.

And for the man.

Awash in mingled longing, joy and sadness, it took her a moment to notice the woman who had suddenly materialized at Preston's side. She was blond, petite and pretty. Beneath her bright red down jacket, she wore a tight, white cowl-necked sweater and jeans that clung to her slender curves like a second skin.

Preston glanced at the woman sharply, frowning, as she wrapped her hand around his arm and went on tiptoe to whisper something in his ear.

He wasn't having any of whatever she was offering. He muttered something out of the side of his mouth and tried to pull free of her grip.

But she held on. And then she whispered something else.

"Let go of my arm, Lucy," he said, each word formed so slowly and deliberately that Belle could read them on his lips. He didn't seem angry, just not the least interested and impatient to escape.

Lucy laughed, the sound forced and brittle. "Oh, now, don't be that way," she teased, too loudly. But she did let go.

Preston took hold of the stroller and rolled it away from her. Belle felt the sweetest cool wash of relief. It was clear he was over his former fiancée.

And beyond relief, she felt…curious. She wanted to know what Lucy might have said to him, which was odd. She'd never been the nosy type. And she was not a jealous person. But for a moment there, when Lucy grabbed his arm, she had most definitely felt the sting of jealousy.

Really, what was happening to her?

She almost smiled. The answer was so obvious.

She *liked* him. She liked him and she wanted him. And already, in the space of six short days, she'd come to care for him. Greatly. She didn't want any other woman to have him.

What she wanted was her chance with him.

Perhaps what she really needed to do was stop running from the urgings of her own heart. She needed to take her sister's advice, to make a play for the tall rancher with the sky-blue eyes.

True, it might not work out. But she would never know unless she tried.

Preston was wheeling Ben in her direction. He never once glanced back at Lucy.

But Belle did. A beefy-looking fellow in a big black hat had grabbed the little blonde by the arm and was pulling her toward the open doors back out to the street. The fellow didn't look happy.

Neither did Lucy. She shook her head and said something Belle couldn't hear. The man just held on to her arm and kept walking, elbowing people aside until he had her through the doors.

Preston reached her side. "That was embarrassing."

She moved in closer. Because she wanted to. Because she was through denying her attraction to him. "You didn't look back."

He shook his head. "No percentage in that." His voice was low, meant just for her. So was the warm light in his eyes.

Still leaning close to him, she said, "You missed the big guy in the black hat. He took her arm and pulled her out of here."

Preston made a low sound in his throat. "That would have been her husband, Monty Polk."

"Ah. I thought as much."

He added, "Monty owns the local car dealership, Polk's Prime Auto. Does real well for himself."

She wanted to ask what Lucy had said to him. And she would. Later. When they were alone.

Ben chose that moment to wake up—with gusto. He

startled and let out a cry of surprise followed by a long, loud wail.

Preston said wryly, "I'm thinking it's about time we headed on home."

Back at the ranch house, Belle said she would change Ben and then get some food in him. Pres went out to check on the horses.

The snow had started in again. After he finished in the stables, he paused in the yard, which was blazing bright with all the Christmas lights. He took off his hat and turned his face to the night sky. He did it just to feel the snow-flakes melting on his cheeks the way he used to do when he was only a kid not that much older than Ben.

It had been a great day. He'd never been much for town events as a rule. And he certainly hadn't seen the appeal of wandering from booth to booth looking at handmade wool hats and frilly aprons and an endless array of Christmas decorations.

But he had Ben now. And Belle was right. A kid needed to feel like part of the community....

Belle. Just thinking her name caused a powerful yearning inside him.

He lowered his head, feeling foolish. He really did need to remember the situation here. She only wanted to help.

And then she would go.

He put on his hat again. Keeping his head down, he returned to the house.

Inside, he washed up quickly at the sink.

Belle took Ben out of his high chair. "Go upstairs with Dada," she said. "He will help you with your bath."

"Dada!" Ben went right into his arms. That was a fine moment to add to his growing collection of them.

Pres carried his son upstairs, bathed him, changed him

and read him the story about what trucks do at night. Ben was already nodding off when Pres put him in his crib and turned out the light.

He left the door open the way Belle always did and followed his nose to the kitchen, where the women had whipped up a meal from what they could find in the fridge. All five of them sat down at the kitchen table to eat and then had coffee and Christmas cookies for dessert.

Once dinner was cleared away, Marcus said good-night. And then Charlotte went across the yard with the old man. She'd said something about the two of them doing a little holiday decorating. But she was fooling nobody. It was just an excuse for them to have some time alone.

Pres tried not to worry that his dad was getting in over his head. Twice before, in the years since they lost his mom, the old man had taken a shine to a female—a nurse who worked at the community hospital and also a widow from a nearby ranch. But those courtships had been brief and his dad was never much beyond lukewarm over either of those women.

It was different with Charlotte. When his dad looked at Belle's companion, his whole face seemed to light up from within. He was totally gone on her. Pres had a feeling it was going to be bad for him when she left. But then again, Charlotte seemed like a fine woman. And it was obvious she was as taken with the old man as he was with her.

Why shouldn't they steal a little happiness while they could? The two of them were old enough by now to know what they were doing. He hoped.

Pres carried his coffee mug to the counter. Belle was loading the last of the dishes into the dishwasher, her sable hair falling forward, the overhead light bringing out the strands of red and gold in the greater mass of rich brown.

Looking at Belle, he kind of got what the old man was

probably going through with Charlotte. Some good things were mighty hard to resist. Belle wore jeans—high-dollar ones of the designer variety—and expensive boots and a pretty gold-colored sweater. Every time he looked at her he wanted to reach out and haul her into his hungry arms.

"I'll take that." She plucked the mug from his hand and put it in the top rack, punched the start button and shut the door. The machine gave a low rumble as the cycle began.

"It was a good day," he said.

"A wonderful day," she agreed. And then, with a strange little smile, she turned and left him there.

He watched her fine backside in those perfect-fitting jeans moving away from him and had to press his lips together to keep from calling her back. It was better that she went. If they hung around downstairs alone together… well, no.

Not a good idea.

He wandered into the family room. Like the rest of the main floor, it was all done up for the holidays, the mantel decked with greenery and lights. From the easy chair by the fire, he could glance over and see a little of the big tree in the front hall.

He put another log on the fire, sat in the easy chair and closed his eyes. Just for a little. In a bit he would turn on the TV, see if he could rustle up a decent movie on pay-per-view.

"Preston." Belle's voice. Soft. A little husky, a *lot* tempting. He had to be dreaming. "Preston…"

He let his eyelids drift open. And then he blinked.

Because she really was right there, standing in front of him, wearing a red robe and red satin slippers. The firelight warmed her smooth skin, brought out the fiery colors in her hair. She really was about the hottest-looking woman he'd ever known. It constantly took him off guard. All that hotness. And yet, she was very ladylike, too—which somehow made her even hotter.

He sat up fast. "Uh. Belle. Yeah?"

She laughed then, tossing her head a little, making the ache within him all the fiercer. "I thought we could spend a little time together. Just the two of us."

He needed to tell her that it wasn't a good idea. But when he opened his mouth, what came out was, "Sure. Have a seat."

She had the baby monitor with her. Setting it on a side table, she took the other easy chair across the fire from him, the silky material of her robe whispering softly, temptingly, as she sat and smoothed the fabric over her knees.

He tried not stare at the curves of her breasts, outlined so perfectly by the clinging robe. Or to look lower, at the long sweep of thigh outlined by the thin robe, the trim ankles peeking out beneath the red hem…

And why hadn't he told her she really ought to get the hell out of there? His brain didn't function properly when she was around—especially not when she was wearing a clingy red robe with very little on underneath it as far as he could tell.

He had to remember that he was trying to stay away from her. As soon as she finished helping him make a life with Ben, she would return to her own world, to her busy life in her glamorous little country, to traveling the globe helping the disadvantaged get decent medical care. The last thing he needed was to fall for her and lose her. He'd been there and done that already.

But no. Not true. He *hadn't* been there. Not by a long shot. Belle was nothing like Lucy. Belle was so much finer, so much truer, so much…more. Losing her would be harder, would hit so much deeper than losing Lucy had. He needed to get up and say good-night and head for the stairs.

But wouldn't you know? He stayed right where he was.

She asked, "So I'm guessing it went well tonight—when you put Ben to bed?"

"It was good. Great. I'm thinking he's getting used to me now, learning to trust me, to feel safe with me."

"I can see that. I'm…glad." She turned and stared at the fire. A log snapped and sparks shot up the chimney. As he watched, she closed her eyes, those thick gold-tipped lashes sweeping down over the high, perfect cheeks. So beautiful. And so sad.

"I'm sorry." The simple words felt scraped out of him.

She sat up straighter, turned her face to him again. Her gaze was steady and she made her mouth turn up in a re-signed smile. "That I'm losing him?"

"Yeah. I…haven't been thinking a lot about how it must be for you."

"That's understandable."

"At first it was just the shock. And the impossibility of it, of having a child I didn't even know about."

"I see that." She arranged that amazing face into a se-rene expression. The serenity didn't quite reach her eyes, however.

He stumbled on. "But now that I'm getting to know him, now I'm starting to believe that I will get to be a real father to him, well, I can't even wrap my mind around how hard it would be if I was the one who would have to walk away."

She smoothed her robe again, the fabric shifting, cling-ing. All at once, his mouth was dry and his Wranglers were way too tight. "It will all work out," she said at last.

He knew he had more to apologize for. "I shouldn't have been so hard on you at the first."

"You couldn't help it."

"You've been nothing but a hero, Belle, about all of this."

Her eyes had the shine of tears in them now. She put

up a slender hand, palm out. "Could we speak of something else?"

He gulped to clear the lump in his throat, reminded himself again that he ought to get up and go *now*. And then he said, "Yeah, sure. Whatever you want…"

She laid her hands on the chair arms, and looked at him from the side, a playful sort of glance. "I saw Lucy whispering to you in the theater today."

He grunted and then grumbled, "Did I mention how embarrassing that was?"

"You did, yes."

He knew what she was after. "You want to know what she said to me."

"I'm not all hero, Preston. Sometimes I want to know things that are none of my business. Just like everyone else."

He thought how he would love to give her…everything. Whatever she wanted. Her heart's desire. Too bad that what he had to offer would never come close to what she had— to who she was—already. "Lucy said she misses me. She wants us to be friends again." He let out a humorless laugh. "I couldn't get clear of her fast enough."

"I noticed that."

"It's all kind of pitiful. I thought my heart was broken when she dumped me for Monty. But now I realize that what was really hurting was only my pride that she chose the car salesman over me. And now, well, it's pretty damn clear she did me a favor. Poor Monty wasn't so lucky. Lucy's turned out to be one of those women who always wants the man she *doesn't* have."

"It's strange the way people are." She spoke in a thoughtful tone. "So many of us are never happy with the life we have. We're just so certain we should have made other choices."

"Are you happy, Belle?" He asked the question before he stopped to think of what it implied. That she *wasn't* happy. That there was something missing from her life.

He knew damn well that wasn't true.

She answered, "Overall, yes. I'm happy. I have a wonderful family, meaningful work to do. I live in a beautiful place. I have good friends—even without Anne, whom I miss terribly."

He wasn't surprised that she found her life satisfying. "No regrets, huh?"

A tiny frown creased the smooth skin of her brow. "I have regrets, yes. That I didn't make more time to be with my friend when she was alive. That I missed out on precious moments we might have spent together. That I..." She seemed to catch herself. "And look where I'm taking this. Into a sad place. I don't want to be sad tonight." Her gaze sought his and held it. He felt the connection powerfully. As though she had reached her soft hand across the distance between them and touched him. "Your house looks beautiful, Preston, all ready for Christmas."

"Because of you." His voice was only a little bit rough.

A ghost of a smile came and went on her lips. "We're going to have to start wrapping some of the gifts we've bought."

"I can't wait," he said, and didn't even roll his eyes.

She seemed to be looking at his mouth. "It's cozy, just you and me by the fire," she said. He said nothing. At that moment, he didn't really trust himself to speak. And then she suggested, "All we need is a little Christmas music...."

"You're serious," he whispered, hardly daring to breathe. It was becoming very clear that she was after more from him tonight than a little friendly conversation.

Why?

Never mind. He didn't care why. When you came right down to it, there was no way he would ever turn her down.

No matter the cost in the end. No matter the eventual pain.

She put her hand against the soft skin just below her throat, where that silky red robe came to together to form a tempting vee. "I am, Preston. I'm serious."

"Then I'll play us some Christmas music." He got up, his arousal increasing with the movement, with the pressure of his zipper against his groin. He knew she could see how easily she excited him. All she had to do was glance at the front of his Wranglers. Normally, that would have shamed him.

But he didn't care if she saw. Let her see. Maybe she'd get smart and leave him alone before this glorious insanity went any further.

She remained in the chair.

He got the remote off the low table by the sofa and turned on the big screen, pulling up the guide, scrolling to the music channels and stopping on the one that played holiday music all through December. Bing Crosby was singing "White Christmas," a song that was old back when his mom and dad were dating.

He put down the remote, returned to her and held down his hand. She took it. He did what he'd dreamed of doing way too often the past few nights. He pulled her up and into his waiting arms.

They danced, slow and sweet, in front of the fire. Neither of them said a word. It was enough, more than he'd ever dared hope for, to have his arms around her, to smell her perfume and feel her silky hair against his chin.

When the song ended, they stopped and swayed together, waiting for the next one to start. It was "The Christmas Song." They began to dance again.

He nuzzled her hair. Because it felt so good and smelled like fresh flowers and cinnamon and some tempting exotic fruit. And he asked, "So what was going on between you and Larry Seabuck today?"

She looked up at him, the firelight dancing in her eyes. "Larry was explaining to me how the bake auction works."

He bent his head enough to brush a kiss against her lips. "Larry has a crush on you. A huge crush."

They were stopped again, swaying together in one place. Her body brushed against his, tempting him. Taunting him. She said, "Not to worry. I have no doubt that RaeNell is going to nip that problem in the bud."

He gathered her just a fraction closer. Nothing like this, not ever in his life: Belle swaying in his arms. "She's a strong-minded woman, that RaeNell. And bossy. She's almost as bossy as Betsy Colson."

She had that irresistible mouth of hers tipped up to him again. "But no one is as bossy as Betsy Colson."

"You got that right." How could he resist kissing her some more? Why would he want to resist? It seemed there was a reason, but now, with her in his arms, he couldn't for the life of him remember what that reason was. He lowered his mouth and settled his lips gently on hers.

She sighed. Her lips parted. He deepened the kiss.

It was a long kiss, lazy and easy and slow. Now and then he would lift his head and slant his mouth the other way and they would go on kissing. He never wanted to stop. It went on through "The Christmas Song" and the next classic song after that.

When that next song was over, she whispered, "Take me upstairs, Preston."

As if he would argue. All those reasons he had for not getting too close to her? He couldn't remember a single one of them now.

He let her go long enough to bank the fire and turn off the music as she went to the side table and got the baby monitor.

They met again by the fire and he kissed her once more, pulling her in to him real snug that time, lost in the taste of her, the feel of her beautiful body all wrapped in red satin under his hands, the scent of her swimming around him, sucking him down into something dark and sweet and too magnificent to bear.

Finally, she pulled away enough to say it again. "Take me upstairs."

He stepped back, offered his hand.

She took it.

Together they turned for the arch to the front hall.

Chapter Nine

They stopped in Ben's room to check on him.

And they ended up standing there by the crib, watching him sleep. The room was in shadow, light slanting in softly from the hallway. When he slid Belle a glance, Pres could see the soft upward curve of her mouth as she gazed at his sleeping son.

He completely understood her fascination with the boy. Ben was a miracle, plain and simple.

It was a gift beyond price, to have a child to raise, a son who would grow up and, God willing, have children of his own. It felt right, felt…solid and true.

And now, for a little while, for this bright and glowing holiday season, not only was there Ben, but there was Belle, too, standing here by the crib beside him. Showing him how to be a father to his son. Showing him goodness. Beauty. And grace. Showing him everything he'd always imagined a woman might be.

And more.

She turned to him, put a hand against his chest, her head tipped down. "Preston," she whispered. Just that. His name.

He put a finger under her chin and lifted her face to him.

And he kissed her, there in the dark beside his son's crib. It was a light kiss. Gentle. She sighed against his lips.

And then he took her hand and led her out of there to the master bedroom, where he turned on the lamp and shut the door.

She set the monitor on the table next to the lamp. He took her arm, loving the feel of her silky robe, of her warm, firm flesh beneath. He pulled her close.

"Preston…" She said his name again, as though she liked saying it, as though she found pleasure at the feel of it on her tongue.

He lowered his mouth and took her lips in a deeper kiss than in the other room, a hungrier kiss. He got a little carried away with it, crushing her to him, loving the feel of her soft breasts against his chest. When they pulled apart that time she gazed up at him wearing a slightly stunned expression, her tempting mouth red and swollen from the kiss.

"I think…" She hesitated. She was looking down again.

He tipped her chin up once more. "Tell me. What?"

She pressed her lips together, sighed. "Well, you know, this is the time when we should speak of contraception, of…protection. You must know that I'm not on the pill. Or anything else." A nervous chuckle escaped her. "I should have planned ahead, shouldn't I? I'm afraid I'm not all that good at this."

"You are doing fine." He meant that. "Better than fine."

"You're kind."

"No." He bent his head, kissed the tip of her delicate nose. "Not kind. Not in the least." Everything about her tempted him. He caught a lock of her hair, rubbed it between his fingers. Warm silk. And then he bent and kissed her again. More slowly, more tenderly. When he lifted his mouth he said, "Don't worry. I have what we need."

"Good." She kissed the side of his throat. The touch of her lips there seemed to burn like a brand.

He took her hand again, led her to the bed. "Stay right there," he instructed, because he still couldn't quite believe she was here in his room with him—that she wouldn't be leaving any second now.

She looked at him so tenderly. "Oh, Preston. Where would I go? I only want to be right here. With you."

"Hold that thought." He turned to the bedside drawer, took out the box of condoms, opened it, set a couple of the little pouches on the table. Then he put the box away. He started to reach for her again.

And then he thought of the bed, that it wasn't ready. That seemed all wrong somehow.

Because he wanted it all to be perfect. Just right. For her...

He cleared his throat, put up a finger. "Just a minute..."

She gave him a trembling smile.

He bent and turned down the bed, smoothing the covers back, revealing the whiteness of pillows and sheets. His damn hands were shaking.

And she saw that they were. She touched his shoulder, whispered his name again. Never in his life had he felt so exposed. "Please..." She said it so gently. He straightened. And she took his arm and turned him to face her. She captured his two hands in her smaller, softer ones and turned them palms up, revealing the worst of the calluses, the scars, the rope burns....

His hands. Her hands. The comparison brought it sharply home again that their lives were worlds apart. "What is it?"

She tipped her head up to him, searched his face. "What's wrong?"

He'd already made a fool of himself, shaking like a newly branded calf right there in front of her. He might as well go ahead and tell her the truth. "My dad was always ready with advice. He taught me that a man should be prepared. So every four years, I buy a fresh box of condoms and throw the old one out."

She gazed up at him, golden-brown eyes full of light and acceptance. "There's nothing wrong with that. That's being responsible."

He put it right out there. "The point is I throw the old condoms away because I've had no occasion to use them."

"Ah," she said, a blush stealing over her cheeks.

"I'm not all that experienced at this, Belle. There was Lucy. And a girl at college. And your friend. And that time, with Anne, well, I told you, I don't even remember it. All we know for sure about that time is that I must have failed to take the old man's advice."

"Oh, Preston." She caught her lower lip between her even white teeth. "You're not going to change your mind about this, are you?"

A low, animal sound escaped him. He pulled his fingers free of hers and caught her face between his rough palms. Her skin was velvet. Perfect. Like the rest of her. "Not on your life."

She breathed a long sigh. "Oh, good."

"It's only…I'm not so smooth. You should know that."

She looked at him trustingly. "I don't care about that. I only want *you.*"

A scary thought occurred to him. "You're not…" He swallowed. Hard. "Belle, is this your first time?"

She shook her head, kissing the pad of his thumb when

it briefly touched her mouth. "There was a man. During my first year at Duke. It didn't last."

He pressed his forehead to hers, closed his eyes. "I just need to know that you're certain about this."

She lifted her mouth to him. "I am." She murmured the two words against his lips.

The temptation was too great. He kissed her again, still holding her sweet face between his hands.

When she opened her eyes and looked at him, he saw no pretense. And no hesitation in her.

She wanted this.

They could have everything. Together. For a little while.

It wouldn't be easy when she left him.

But he would think about that later, deal with that later, when the time came.

Her hands were on his chest again, as if she sought his heartbeat beneath the fabric of his wool shirt. And then her fingers got busy, undoing the buttons, top to bottom.

He helped her, pulling the shirttails free of his Wranglers as she skimmed the heavy shirt off his shoulders and tossed it to a nearby chair. Underneath, he wore a white T-shirt. She kissed him, through the T-shirt, in the center of his chest. And then she eased the T-shirt out from under his belt and up over his belly.

"Lift your arms," she commanded.

He obeyed. She tossed the T-shirt on the chair, too. Laughing a little, she kicked off those pretty little red slippers of hers. Oh, she was something, so eager and so sweet.

"Strong…" Her voice was husky, low. A seduction in itself. She did it again, laid her hands flat against his chest, which was bare, now. "So hot…" She stroked him, traced the trail of hair down the center of him to where it disappeared under his belt. He got even harder.

If that was possible.

She undid the belt, took it away.

He let her do all the work. He should have been more forceful, he supposed. Should have taken the lead.

But she seemed so pleased with herself, unsnapping and unzipping and whipping all his clothes away, pushing him down to take off his boots, then pulling him up to his feet again. He let her do it. All of it.

And when he didn't have a stitch left, she cuddled up nice and close to him. She kissed him. For a long, slow time. She wrapped her arms around him and rubbed his back, those naughty soft fingers trailing downward, to the base of his spine, lower....

She even eased her hand between them and wrapped her fingers around him. He groaned when she did that. And then she tried a slow stroke. He groaned again, deeper and harder than the first time.

That smooth hand sliding over him, gripping him nice and tight...it was almost more than he could bear. He was getting mighty close to finishing before they even really got started. He needed to step up a little, claim some control, or he would lose it completely before they even made it down to the bed, lose it just from the sweet encircling pressure of her tender hand.

He caught her wrist, squeezed it a little. She took his signal and let him go. He lifted her hand to his lips, kissed her fingers one by one. And then he guided that hand around behind her and hauled her up so close and tight, she let out a tiny gasp, a sweet little breathless sound.

Another kiss. He couldn't get enough of those kisses of hers. Sweet as honey. Hot as flame.

And so they kissed. And kissed some more.

She still had that robe on. And whatever skimpy little lacy things were under it.

He really wanted to see that, the lace and the satin under

there. To see what she had against her skin. But he wanted to stretch out the anticipation, too. He was aching to have her, but he wanted to make it last.

Her robe came together in that tempting vee between the soft swells of her breasts. He traced it with his finger. She gazed up at him, her eyes so wide open to him he could have fallen inside them, inside *her,* could have been melted down to nothing in amber fire.

He meant to go lower, get the tie end of the satin belt and give it a pull. The belt would drop away—and the robe would fall open. That was the plan.

But her breasts were too tempting. They distracted him. He guided the robe out of the way—on one side and then the other, the fabric giving, pulling up out of the belt to expose her breasts to his hungry gaze.

She had a little bit of silk and lace over them—not a bra, but a very short little sliplike thing that came to her waist and was pulling out of the belt a little. He could see her nipples underneath that bit of silk, see the exact puckered shape of them, so sweet and tight. The sight sent more heat burning through his groin. He was so hard it hurt now. A glorious kind of pain.

"What's this?" he asked, brushing a thumb over the lace, slipping a finger down the tiny satin strap that held it up.

"Camisole," she replied.

He repeated the word, gruffly, "Camisole…" He probably should have known that.

She was probably thinking he really needed to get out more.

And why shouldn't she think that?

After all, it was true.

And how could he help himself? He bent, put his mouth over the tip of one breast, right over the silky fabric of the camisole. He stuck out his tongue, used his teeth to tease her through the silk, to make that nipple harder still.

She let out a soft cry and reached for him, threading her fingers up into his hair, bringing his head down even closer, pushing her breasts up to him. An offering.

One he gladly accepted. He moved to the other breast, gave it the same treatment as he had the first.

And after that, he forgot all about how he wanted to undress her slowly, to peel away the layers, to take his sweet time.

He had the tie end of the belt in his fingers and he pulled. It fell away. He eased the silky robe off her shoulders. It collapsed with a soft little whoosh to the rug. And then he was grabbing the hem of the camisole. She raised her arms and he took it up and off her.

Heaven. Heaven under there, soft and pink and perfect. He had never seen such beauty. Her skin had that wonderful luster to it. The scent of her drove him wild.

He swept his hands down the slim curve of her back, over her perfect, round bottom, scooping her up, lifting her—and then laying her gently down, sideways, on the turned-back bed. He eased her thighs apart and moved between them, still standing, his feet planted on the bedside rug.

She had on tiny little red panties. He hooked his fingers under the bits of elastic where they hugged her slim hips, and he pulled. She raised her long legs high so he could slide them off.

Careful. Gentle. The words echoed in his brain. He didn't want to hurt her or be too rough with her.

But much stronger than the warnings in his head as to how to treat a lady was the hunger, the need for her that pounded in his blood. He tossed the panties over his shoulder and guided her raised legs open again, around him. She sighed.

He bent over her. Her mouth was waiting. He took it, cradling her head, her hair falling over his arm, brushing him with the warmth of living silk. He speared his tongue inside, past her open lips, relearning all those silky surfaces in there, where it was hot and wet and tasted of paradise.

She moaned into his mouth.

He drank the sound, as he drank the sweet, intoxicating taste of her. And as he kissed her, he touched her. From those perfect, round breasts, down over her smooth, flat belly—and lower.

She cried out when he cupped her mound. She cried out and she lifted herself toward him, welcoming him, offering him more.

Everything.

All of her...

He couldn't wait. He moved his fingers, parting her.

More silk. Hot silk. And so wet. He stroked her and she moved against his hand, pushing her body toward him, driving him crazy with wanting her.

Last, he reminded himself, dizzy with the wonder of her. *Make it last...*

He groaned and he kept kissing her as he sought and found the heart of her pleasure. She lifted up on her elbows to kiss him more deeply, gasping into his mouth when he moved his thumb around that most sensitive spot. He focused on that, narrowing his attention down to that tiny core.

It didn't take long. Within a few short, beautiful moments, she was going over. He felt the tiny, rhythmic pulsing of her climax against his hand.

She whispered his name and collapsed back across the bed.

He wasted no time. Grabbing the condom from the bedside table, he tore off the wrapper and rolled it into place.

She gazed up at him, her eyes bigger, deeper than ever, her body limp, her beautiful skin dewy, flushed.

Still standing above her, he bent again to lift her, rearranging her, so her head was cradled on the pillows. She moved where he put her, his to command.

His.

It was true. For now, she *was* his. And now was what mattered. Now. Tonight. Tomorrow. And the next day. The few magical days she would stay with him.

It was enough for him.

Because it would have to be.

She lifted those slender arms to him. "Preston, come here. Closer, here, to me…"

The mattress shifted as he joined her, easing himself between her smooth thighs, lowering his body to hers with great care, trying not to crush her, not to smother her with his greater bulk and weight.

She was braver, wilder, bolder. She wrapped her arms and legs around him, pulling him to her. Reaching down between them, she clasped him. He let out a strangled sound as she guided him into place.

His mind spun away. He forgot to be careful. There was only the pleasure, only the feel of her as he sank into her waiting heat.

She…surrounded him, took him, *owned* him completely. She was so sweet and tight. Dangerous. Wonderful. His very own princess.

For tonight.

For a while.

But he wasn't going to think about time limits now.

About losing her. About later. About how it would be when this sweet insanity was over.

Right now, he could almost believe that this, the two of them, was forever. That what they'd found together was so special, so good, so true and real and right that it couldn't end.

It *wouldn't* end.

She pulled him down and he went, gladly. He couldn't stop himself. Couldn't hold himself back. Not now. Not anymore. He surged into her. She lifted those slender legs higher, tighter around him, hitching them behind him, pulling him closer, deeper still.

Her mouth was under his, her tongue boldly sweeping the surfaces beyond his lips. He was lost in a tossing, stormy sea of sensation. Her skin. His skin. Her mouth, his. He moved within her and she took him, claimed him, branded him.

She gave his own need back to him, her eagerness and willingness somehow amplifying every frantic, hungry thrust.

He tried to slow it down, to take control again. But he had no control. There was only Belle, her body holding his, her arms so close around him, her legs squeezing him tight, drawing him down deeper and deeper into her, into the sweetness, into the heat and the softness of her.

They moved as one, rocking together, spiraling deeper and deeper into a velvet darkness, a darkness that split wide open at the end into blazing-hot, blinding light.

Chapter Ten

Belle woke when the bed shifted. She was smiling as she opened her eyes. The room was dark and Preston's tall shadow loomed above her.

"What are you doing?" She covered her wide yawn with the back of her hand. "What time is it?"

He was already out of the bed, but he paused and bent close to her again. With those big, gentle hands of his, he tucked the covers closer around her in a way that made her feel cared-for—cherished. "It's a little before five," he whispered. "Go back to sleep."

"But where are you going?" She dragged herself up against the pillows and turned on the lamp by her side of the bed.

He was sticking his feet into his jeans. "Morning chores. They don't wait." He zipped them up and sent her a glance that held all the wonder of the night before within it. "Not even for a man lucky enough to have you in his bed...."

Oh my, he was one fine figure of a man. Just looking at his broad shoulders, at the hard muscles of his long arms, she felt quivery and warm inside, love struck and very young. It would be so lovely to simply lie here in his bed and wait for his return.

But then she thought of Ben, of the real reason she was here, in this house, with this man. There was much in the world beyond her own selfish pleasure. And sometimes it was simply wiser to maintain a certain pretense of decorum. For now, at least, it was probably smarter to keep their new relationship private, just between the two of them.

She said, "I should probably go down the hall to my own bed anyway."

He pulled on his white T-shirt. And then, for several sweet, endless seconds, he just stood there gazing at her. "You're something special. I still can't believe it, that you're here. In this room. With me." He whispered the words.

She wanted to leap from the bed and throw herself into his arms again. But there would time for that.

Tonight. The word whispered through her, full of promise. Once Ben was in bed and Marcus had retreated to his room off the kitchen and Charlotte came up with yet another excuse to visit Silas across the yard, it would be just the two of them. They could be together. In every way.

He was on the move again, putting on his heavy shirt, buttoning it up. She sat, all warm and cozy under the covers, and watched him as he buckled his belt, dropped to the chair by the window and pulled on his socks and his boots.

"Breakfast," she commanded, as he turned for the door. "Seven-thirty. Be there." Some days he didn't come in until after nine or ten and some days he and Silas took food with them and didn't return until afternoon.

"Yes, ma'am." He sent her one last lovely, intimate glance and then he was gone.

* * *

Pres came in for breakfast as he'd promised Belle he would. He washed up fast and then joined the rest of them at the kitchen table, taking the empty seat between Belle's chair and Ben's high chair.

"Good morning." He gave Belle a grin he hoped didn't reveal too much.

"Good morning." Her answering smile was merely cordial. The look in her eyes, however, made him want to leap up and haul her high against his chest and carry her up the stairs and straight to his bed again.

Ben made a gurgly sound. "Hi, Dada!"

And that reminded him to stop staring at her like he wanted to gobble her whole, to turn to his son. "Hi, Ben. How are you this morning?"

Ben answered him in a long string of enthusiastic nonsense syllables, after which he picked up a handful of dry cereal, stuffed it in his mouth and chewed.

Pres said, "Good to hear it, son," as Charlotte appeared at his shoulder with the coffeepot. "Thank you," he told her. She filled his mug, then went around the table topping off cups.

When she sat back down, they started passing the bowls of scrambled eggs and sausage, the platters of flapjacks, the butter and the warmed maple syrup. It was their usual Sunday breakfast.

"Silas," said Charlotte in an admiring tone, "you weren't joking. You really can cook."

The old man looked proud as a turkey gobbler in a hen pen. "A man ought to be able to iron his own shirts, fry up a mess of sausage and scramble a dozen eggs at the very least, I always say."

Marcus, silent as usual, looked from Charlotte to Silas,

eyes narrowed. And then he glanced at Belle, after which he looked straight at Pres.

Pres got the picture. The bodyguard knew everything. He knew about Charlotte and Silas. And he knew where Her Highness Arabella had spent most of last night.

Did Belle know that Marcus knew? Would it matter to her? After all, it was the bodyguard's job to keep her safe. *And* to keep her secrets.

Pres didn't like it. He didn't understand it—the kind of life where you needed a professional soldier protecting you constantly. It was just another example of the vast difference between her world and his, more proof that he was living in a fantasy with her. And another indication that there was no way this amazing thing between them could ever go anywhere.

And as long as he kept that in mind, well, there was no problem, right? He wouldn't let himself go getting ideas. He would enjoy this time with her.

And not start expecting there to be more.

Beside him, Belle spoke. "We should keep the time in mind. We don't want to be late for nine o'clock Mass. I was thinking we could take two vehicles as usual. Preston can drive Ben and me. Silas and Charlotte, you can ride with Marcus."

"What the hell?" groused the old man at full volume. "Leave me out of it. I'm not a churchgoing man. I haven't set foot in a damn church since Pres's mother passed."

Ben, in his high chair, stared wide-eyed. "Pawpaw." He put his little index finger against his lips. "Shh."

Charlotte said quietly, "Silas, language. The child…"

The old man sputtered some more, but he did tone it down a tad. "I'm just saying I ain't going, that's all."

Charlotte clucked her tongue. "Of course you are."

"No, Shar, I'm not."

Shar. He was calling her *Shar* now? Pres couldn't resist sliding a glance at Belle to see her reaction. She was playing it downright demure, carefully slicing a bite of sausage, bringing it delicately to her lips, chewing with slow, measured care.

"As I recall," Charlotte reminded his father in a fond, indulgent tone, "just yesterday afternoon you stood right there on Main Street and told that lovely Deluca couple that you *would* be at Sunday Mass."

The old man made a huffing noise. "Pres told them. I didn't say a thing. People can make up their minds to whatever they want as far as I'm concerned. That doesn't mean I have to do what they decide is good for me."

"But it isn't *for* you, specifically," Charlotte said gently. And she tipped her head in Ben's direction. "Silas," she added. "Please." That was all. Just the old man's name. Softly. With that ladylike "please" right after it.

His father huffed and grunted and knocked back a big slug of coffee. He set the cup down harder than he needed to. "All right. Okay. Sunday Mass. Why not?"

When they reached the pretty white Church of the Immaculate Conception, Pres and Belle took Ben to the nursery provided for the youngest children. They kissed Ben goodbye and told him they would be back soon. He waved at them, opening and closing his hand in their direction the way he liked to do, but he didn't make any fuss at all. So they left him there with two pretty teenagers, both of whom seemed affectionate and attentive with the kids they would be looking after.

Mass was short. Nobody in their group took communion. Did they all have unconfessed sins, then? Pres had a pretty good idea of what his father's and Charlotte's sins might be. And he knew his own and Belle's intimately. He had no idea what sins Marcus needed forgiving for—if any. Strange, to think of the bodyguard that way, as someone with baggage like everyone else.

A man. A sinner.

Marcus seemed much too self-contained and disciplined to have any sins to account for.

Pres spotted Lucy and Monty a few rows in front of them. He was careful not to waste any time looking at them. The last thing he needed was for Lucy to try and catch his eye—let alone for Monty to see her doing it.

Belle sat beside him. He couldn't keep from stealing frequent glances at her. She was the most beautiful creature he'd ever seen. And since last night, to him, she seemed even more beautiful than ever—if it was possible for her to get any better looking than she'd been before. He loved the fine, pure line of her profile, the way her hair caught the light, reflecting copper glints in the shaft of sun coming in the stained-glass window at the end of their pew.

Once or twice, she turned and saw him staring. She didn't seem bothered by his gaping at her like a lovesick puppy. Each time she caught him looking, she gave him a secret, tender smile, a smile meant just for him. A smile that only made him want to stare at her some more.

He kept reminding himself to get a grip. And he would. For a few minutes, he would pay attention to the droning of the priest. And then he would find himself turning her way again, getting hypnotized by the perfect curve her chin, the smooth line of her throat. He would be dazzled by the sight of the sun on her hair.

After the service, the Delucas asked them to come on over to the Sweet Stop for lunch. Pres was thinking he ought to get back. He had a sick mare he wanted to look in on.

But all of a sudden the old man was Mr. Sociable. "A

fine suggestion, John. Don't you think so, Shar? Lunch sounds mighty fine about now. After a generous helping of religion, I like a nice big burger and a jumbo order of fries at least as much as the next man." He accepted the invitation for the rest of them.

And why not? Pres found himself thinking.

A man needed to eat.

They caravanned over to the diner, which was packed with the after-church crowd. It took an hour to get a table.

They didn't get back to the ranch until after three. Ben was fast asleep in his car seat by then.

When he stopped the quad cab and turned off the engine, Belle asked, "Shall I take him in?"

He indulged himself and looked at her again. She'd made him crazy all day long with wanting to touch her, to kiss her, to be free to wrap his arm around her and have everyone in town know that she was with him.

What would that be like, to have Belle at his side every day for the rest of his life? To sleep beside her in his bed every night? There was a dream worth dying for.

A dream the likes of him was never going to make into reality.

He knew that, he reminded himself for the thousandth time. He accepted that.

He leaned close to her across the console between their seats, drawn as if by a magnet. He had treated windows in the cab, so it wasn't all that easy to see them in there. Plus, the others were already filing into the house, not even looking their way. "God, you're so beautiful...."

She gave him that smile again, that little secret one that made him want to grab her close and never let her go. "Oh, Preston..."

He loved the way she said his name, making it sound both formal and intimate at the same time. Because he couldn't stop himself, he leaned in even closer and captured her mouth. He tasted her soft lips, felt her sweet breath across his skin.

With great effort, he made himself pull away and answer her original question. "No. It's all right. I'll get him."

He got out of the truck. The car seat was on the driver's side, so Pres opened that door and leaned in to unhook the sleeping kid from the seat.

Ben woke with a start. He blinked furiously and then let out an ear-flaying shriek. "Mama! Mama…" He looked all around him, frantic. "Mama, Mama!"

Stunned, Pres just stood there, holding the hook end of the seat restraint, as Ben waved his arms and screamed some more. "No, Dada. Mama. Mama…."

Belle touched his shoulder. "Here. Let me…" She sounded unruffled. Not shocked in the least by Ben's sudden outburst.

Pres dropped the restraint belt. He couldn't jump aside fast enough. "All right. Yeah. Please…"

Ben kept screaming, calling for Anne as Belle calmly eased the restraint over his head and pulled him from the seat. She hugged him close, kissed his cheek and murmured gentle reassurances, even though he kept flailing and struggling and crying for his mama. Pres would have sold his soul about then, to have the power to bring Anne Benton back, to give the boy what he wanted so desperately.

But Anne was never coming back.

And when Belle left, if this happened, he was damn well going to have to be ready to step up and deal. "Here, let me take him."

She frowned over Ben's squirming body at him.

He spoke again, levelly, "It's okay. Let me…"

"No, no, no, Dada. No, Belle. Mama, Mama!" Ben

screamed even louder as Belle passed him to Pres. "No, Dada, no!"

"Tell him it's all right…" She held his eyes, spoke in an even tone.

Pres got to work on that. "Shh, Ben. Ben, it's okay. Mama's not here. Mama can't come, but you're safe. You're all right. We…love you." Damn. Was that the first time he'd said that? He said it again. "We love you so much. You're safe. It's okay.…"

Ben wasn't convinced. He went on wailing, flailing his fists, shaking his head. Snot flew and tears streamed down his hot, flushed cheeks. Pres just held on, as gently as he could, and went on babbling about how it was okay and how Ben was safe.

Slowly, the small body relaxed and the cries grew less frantic. In the end, with a watery hiccup and a sad little sigh, Ben leaned his head on Pres's shoulder. "Dada," he said, the word a sort of surrender. His body still quivered with the aftershocks of his outburst. Pres cradled him closer, pressed his lips against his sweaty temple, rubbed his back—and followed Belle into the house.

She hung her heavy coat on the hall tree and then led the way upstairs. By the time they got to Ben's room, the kid was conked out, fast asleep.

"Naptime," Belle whispered. She left the room.

Pres knew what to do. He carried the limp little body to the changing table and got him out of his coat and winter clothes. Belle returned with a warm, damp cloth. She handed it over and he gently, with great care, washed Ben's tear-stained face.

His diaper had a load in it. Pres made short work of cleaning it up and putting on a fresh one. He snapped him into a footed, long-sleeved baby union suit—what Belle called a onesie.

When he put him in the crib and covered him with a blanket, Ben didn't even open his eyes. Pres stood over him, watching him, ready to scoop him up and hold him close if he woke up and started in screaming again.

But nothing happened. The hot flush had left his innocent cheeks. He slept the deep sleep of the safe and the blameless.

Belle turned on the monitor base and grabbed the receiver. They went out to the hall, where he caught her free hand and pulled her into his room.

He took her in there and shut the door, then shucked off his winter coat and his Sunday jacket. He tossed them both across a chair. "What *was* that?" He sank to another chair by the window. "Is he all right? Is he…" He hardly knew what to ask her, didn't know where to begin.

She remained at the door, her back against it, leaning on it, as though Ben's fit of crying had worn her out, too. "He's as all right as can be expected, given that he lost his mother sixteen days ago."

"Sixteen days…" It was no time at all. He should have remembered that. It was so easy to forget, because he'd hardly known Anne, hadn't seen her in two and a half years. Sometimes it was hard to keep in mind how recently she'd been lost to those who loved her.

Belle lifted her proud chin. "Already, he's healing. Forgetting her. You can see that in the way he behaves most of the time now. Sunny-natured, happy, curious and sweet."

"It hurts you." He could see it in her eyes, in the trembling of her mouth as she spoke of her friend. "That Anne is fading from his memory."

She gave a brave little shrug. "It's part of who we are, as a species, to learn to forget. It's survival. When we're small, we're so vulnerable. All we know then is to bond with the ones who care for us. Ben's…mechanism for memory isn't really formed yet. He's letting her go as he's meant to do, and bonding with you. With Silas. As he's already bonded with Charlotte and me. But now and then, something triggers him. The last few times, it's been when he suddenly woke from a sound sleep. He wakes up and he…seems to remember her, to know that she's not there."

"You think maybe he's been dreaming about her?"

"Perhaps. That makes sense. But whatever triggers him, he's flung back to needing his mother, the one he knew first. And then he cries for her to come and comfort him. Anne…" Her voice caught. She coughed to clear her throat. "Anne was a fine mother, Preston."

He raked his fingers back through his hair. "I have no doubt." His voice sounded raggedy to his own ears, rough with all the things he didn't exactly know how to say.

"I think that was the worst thing of all for her, about dying so young, to have to leave Ben behind." She shut her eyes, drew in a breath and then finally looked at him again. "I suppose that's every mother's worst nightmare, to go away forever and leave a helpless child behind."

He rose. "And this…this bonding thing that babies do. That's one of the reasons you got here so fast, brought my son to me not even a week after his mother was in the ground. So he wouldn't have to get too…attached to you and then lose you, too."

She swallowed, hard. "Yes," she said on a bare breath's worth of sound.

"You brought him right quick, even though no one would have faulted you if you had waited a little, kept him to yourself a while longer."

"*I* would have faulted me. It wouldn't have been right."

He had no words then. Sometimes words were just a bunch of pointless noise anyway. He ate up the floor between them in four long strides. She watched him come to her, those eyes huge and haunted. He reached for her and she fell against him with a soft, surrendering sigh, her slim arms sliding around his waist.

And he held her, wanting somehow to soak up all her hurts into his own flesh, to take them away from her, into himself.

A careful tap on the door behind her had them pulling apart. Belle stepped to the side, smoothing her hair and straightening the front of her suit jacket.

He opened the door enough to stick his head through. "Yeah?"

Charlotte gave him a prim little smile. "We were worried about Ben…."

It began to seem a little ridiculous, peering at her through the crack in the door. She had to have figured out that Belle was in the room with him. He pulled the door wide, so the women could see each other and he said, "We were just talking about Ben."

"Ah." Charlotte's expression was neutral, those prominent eyes giving nothing away. "Is he all right, then?"

Belle was nodding. "He's fine now." She gestured across the hall at Ben's open bedroom door. "As you can see, he's fast asleep."

"Good. I just thought I ought to come up and…" Charlotte waved her hand in a gesture that said she couldn't figure out how to go on.

Belle told her softly, "Thank you, Charlotte. We're fine."

"All right, then. We will see you downstairs."

"Yes, we'll be right there."

With a nod, Charlotte turned and left them.

As soon as she disappeared from view, Pres shut the door again. This time, he was the one who leaned on it. He folded his arms across his chest and shook his head. "That was awkward."

Belle chuckled. The sound lifted his spirits. She didn't seem so sad and wounded anymore. "Charlotte is very perceptive. She's also the soul of discretion. And she never presumes."

Pres translated. "You mean she knows about us, but she won't make judgments or shoot her mouth off."

"Precisely."

"How does she know?" he asked carefully.

She gave him a patient look. "I didn't tell her, if that's what you're asking. We haven't discussed what happened in this room last night. And yet, I do believe she knows."

"Yeah, well. And *we* know about her and the old man."

"Yes, Preston, we do."

He confessed, "I worry about the old man a little, that he's getting carried away with her."

"Perfectly understandable," she said lightly. "Because Charlotte, after all, is a dangerous seductress." She was joking, he got that.

He just didn't think it was all that funny. "I don't want him to get hurt is all."

"I could say the same for Charlotte. But then I remind myself that she is a mature adult and more than capable of making her own decisions about her life and about love."

"Love?" He said it a little too strongly and he knew it, a little too accusingly.

She gave an elegant shrug. "Or…romance or relationships. Whatever you would prefer to call it. Charlotte's relationships are her own affair. I trust her judgment absolutely."

He looked at her sideways, thinking that she was way too smart and sophisticated for a man like him. And too beautiful. He wanted to touch her, to pull her close again. But if he put his hands on her now, it wouldn't be to comfort her.

Which was why he wasn't going to reach for her. Now

was hardly the time to be thinking about getting her out of that pretty blue church suit of hers. The others were waiting for them downstairs.

He kept his arms folded across his chest. "You lecturing me, Your Highness?"

"Let's just say I am reminding you that what is between Charlotte and your father is not for us to judge."

When she talked like that, all prissy and correct, it got him hot—but then, *whatever* she did, it got him hot. And that bugged him because he knew that what he *should* do was call a dead halt to this thing that was going on between them. He knew he should stop it with her—and he also knew that as long as she was in his house, he wasn't going to be able to keep away from her. Not as long as she was willing.

And she *was* willing. Even as she lectured him, he could see his own desire reflected in those golden-brown eyes, see how much alike they were deep down—even though they belonged in different worlds. Both careful people. Controlled.

Until now. With each other.

With her, especially since last night, he felt he teetered on the brink of losing control.

Feeling on the verge of losing it made him hotter still. In a minute, if he didn't rein himself in a little, she'd be asking him if he had a gun in his pocket.

To keep from grabbing her, he taunted, "And your bodyguard knows about you and me, too. Were you aware of that?"

She didn't turn a hair. "It is Marcus's job to know such things. And like Charlotte, he is the soul of discretion."

"The soul of discretion," he echoed in a growl.

She drew her slim shoulders up. "That is what I said."

"The point is, he knows about us and it's none of his damn business."

"Of course it's his business. That we are lovers concerns him directly. It's his task to protect me. That means he must stay close to me. And *that* means he will have to know things about me and my…activities that no one else knows. The point, though, is that he is trustworthy and discreet and will only use what he knows in the furtherance of his job as my bodyguard."

"Wow, you said a mouthful." He laid on the sarcasm— and yeah, okay, he should back the hell off. He knew it. She was not the enemy. But this whole situation was eating at him. Every time he touched her, it only made him want her more. And where could it go? Nowhere.

She said, "I'm only trying to make you see that Marcus will keep my secrets. And yours as well."

"I don't like it."

"Your preference is duly noted," she replied, so proper and prissy, it made him long to snatch her up and throw her on the floor and have his evil way with her, right then and there.

He muttered darkly, "Around these parts, the women don't need some hired man living off the kitchen to protect them."

Those amber eyes flashed real fire. She opened her mouth to come right back at him—but then she shut it without saying a word. She gave him a long, searching look. And then she asked him quietly, "What's happened? Why are you so angry? What did I do?"

Shame flooded him.

She had only ever treated him with respect and honesty and tenderness. He had no right to go getting up in her face because she trusted her companion and had confidence in the ethics of her bodyguard.

He made himself answer truthfully, "I'm not angry. I just want to kiss you so bad it hurts. And now's not the time for kissing and I feel like the biggest damn fool in Montana. I…" He forgot whatever he was going to say next.

Because she stepped right up and into his arms.

Chapter Eleven

"Then kiss me," she said.

Her mouth was right there, inches below his. She smelled of flowers and wonderful, sweet spices he didn't know the names of. And beneath her perfume: woman. All woman.

He tried to remember all the reasons that kissing her now was not a good idea. "We have to—" She cut him off by surging up and sealing his lips with her own.

That did it.

He hauled her even closer, banding his yearning arms tight around her, lifting her feet right off the floor. She opened beneath the hot push of his tongue. He tasted the sweet wetness within. His pulse was pounding, his blood roaring in his ears.

Never ever in his life had he felt like this. He wasn't… that kind of man.

The kind who took without thinking. The kind who let himself lose control.

She lifted her legs and hooked her dressy little boots around his waist. The roaring in his blood got louder, it blocked out everything but the primal need to be with her.

Joined with her.

All at once he was reeling, kissing her without end, carrying her, all wrapped tight around him, to the bed.

They fell across it, mouths still fused, her pinned-up hair coming loose, tangling between them, catching in the beard shadow on his cheeks, caressing his throat.

They rolled, their hands all over each other, unzipping, unbuttoning, tugging up and away. She took down his zipper, kicked off the short boots she wore. He heard them go flying.

He hadn't thought to lock the door. It was crazy and stupid. But that didn't make it any less urgent, any less absolutely necessary.

She had on tights. Pantyhose. Whatever women called those things. But she hiked up that slim skirt without a second thought and shimmied them down. He pulled them off the rest of the way.

He touched her there, at the womanly core of her. Wet. Hot. Ready.

She moaned as he stroked her, rocking her hips against his hand.

He absolutely had to be inside her. And she was reaching for him, pulling him down. He took her mouth again and below, he touched her some more, stroking the velvet-slick secret flesh, seeking the center of her pleasure. He found it. She cried out. He took the sound into himself. He drank that cry.

"Please." The word passed from her into him. And again, "Please…" She reached down between them, found him, wrapped her fingers around him and guided him home.

At the last possible second before he buried himself in

her, the all-important word appeared in his reeling brain: condom. With a groan of pure agony, he jerked his hips back. She moaned in protest and tried to pull him to her again.

"Wait. Condom," he somehow managed to tell her. He made low, reassuring sounds as he reached for the bedside drawer.

"Contraception." She breathed the word against his lips. "So inconvenient." She laughed into his mouth. The low, teasing sound ricocheted inside his skull. She had one hand around the back of his neck, holding the kiss, holding *him*. Her soft, clever fingers sifted up into his hair. Her other hand remained between them, encircling him, stroking, driving him out of what was left of his mind....

He lifted up enough to glare at her. "We shouldn't even be doing this."

"Oh, yes." Her eyes were so deep. Oceans of amber. So deep, so impossibly soft. "We *should*. We absolutely should...." She tried to pull his mouth down on hers again.

"Wait..." And at last his fumbling fingers closed over the box of condoms in the open drawer. Somehow, he got the top flap back, pulled one out. He ripped the package open with his teeth.

She helped him then, taking the opened pouch from him, removing the condom and then easing both hands between them to neatly roll it on.

"There." She gazed up at him, shameless. Beautiful. Waiting.

How did he get so lucky?

She held up her arms.

He went down to her, claiming her mouth again, burying himself in her with one quick, sure stroke. She gasped. They stilled, the world centering down to only the two of them, only this magic that would not be denied.

Finally, she lifted her legs to wrap them around him. He surged into her harder. Deeper.

Everything flew away. There was this moment and it was endless. They moved together toward the heart of the fire.

When his climax shuddered through him, she held him tight. She pressed her body up to him, giving him everything, making it last. And then, finally, she joined him, all that wet, hot sweetness, pulsing around him.

She said his name, "Preston," soft and low and tender. And her body went loose and easy beneath him.

Belle couldn't believe what had just happened: urgent, amazing sex in the middle of the afternoon. She'd never done anything like it before. She hadn't known what she was missing.

"I don't think we locked the door," she whispered as she tried to catch her breath.

"Nope." He was breathless, too. "We didn't." He kissed her temple, his lips so soft and warm, and he smoothed her wildly tangled hair.

She laughed low. "Oh, we are very, very bad."

He caught her face between his big, rough, tender hands. And he kissed her mouth again. "It's not funny." But in those blue eyes she saw the spark of humor he was trying to hide.

And she thought how never ever in her life before had anything felt so right, so good, so exactly suited to her as this man—as being with this man.

She gazed up into those sunny-day eyes and she knew, right then. At that moment.

I love him.

The room all at once seemed suffused with light.

But only for a second or two. Then her more logical self prevailed.

She'd known him for exactly one week. He belonged here, was rooted here, on this land, in this harsh and beautiful northern state in the brash, young country where her father had been born. He wasn't going to leave Montana, would not walk away from his horses, from his family ranch. She knew that in her soul.

If she chose him—and if he chose her in return—her life would change dramatically. She would be a rancher's wife.

She waited to be horrified at the very idea.

But she wasn't horrified. Instead she felt…excited. Anticipatory.

If I married him, I could stay here, with him. And with Ben. In this lovely little town, in this big, sturdy house…

All right. So the thought of moving here did hold a certain appeal. At least it did right now. And she could still do the work that mattered to her. She could travel when necessary, could still speak up for those in need. There might even be important causes right here in Montana to which she could contribute a helpful voice.

But she didn't have to leap straight to forever-after. They could take a little time over this, see how it went in the next couple of weeks, see if this thing that felt like love right now got stronger.

There was no downside to giving the two of them more time to know each other, more time to discover if they could be a team in a forever kind of way.

Yes, she might be a hopeless romantic who had always dreamed of finding just the right man for her.

And Preston might very well be that man.

But they had weeks yet, together, here in this house, in this fine, rugged land he called home.

He was a careful man in many ways. And cautious. He

would probably be scared out of his wits if she announced right now, out of the blue, that she loved him.

In fact, he was already starting to look a little anxious. "Belle? What is it? What's the matter?"

She laughed again and pulled him closer and kissed him slow and deep and sure. "Nothing's the matter," she said when he lifted away to frown down at her. "On the contrary, things right now are just about perfect."

"If you keep looking at me like that, we'll never pull ourselves together and get downstairs."

"So true. And then they will be certain that we're up here doing exactly what we *have* been doing. But then again, they're probably already certain."

He kissed her once more, hard and quick, then he pushed himself away and stood. "We need to go down there."

Her skirt was still up around her waist. His Sunday trousers were all in a wad down on his boots.

From the waist up, they were both fully dressed, although more than a bit rumpled. He turned away long enough to dispose of the condom, after which he pulled up his trousers. Tucking in his shirt, he zipped and buttoned and hooked his belt.

She sighed and put a hand to her tousled head. "I'm going to need a few minutes to pull myself together."

He held down a hand. She took it and rose to stand with him. So sweetly and tenderly, he smoothed her skirt back down. "Go ahead, then. I have to change into work clothes anyway. Once we're both ready, we can go down together."

Pres stopped in the kitchen with Belle before he went out to check on the sick mare. It didn't seem right to leave her to face the others alone after what the two of them had been doing up in his room.

But it turned out to be no big deal. His dad, who'd

changed from his Sunday clothes into jeans and an ancient sweatshirt, sat at the table reading the Sunday issue of the *Elk Creek Gazette.* Charlotte, wearing one of Doris's aprons, stood at the counter cutting up vegetables. Marcus was nowhere in sight.

"Need some help?" Belle asked her companion.

Charlotte looked over with a warm smile. "I just popped that lovely rib roast Doris left for us into the oven. Feel like peeling potatoes?"

"I would adore peeling some potatoes."

The old man didn't even look up from his newspaper.

Pres said, "Well, I'll head on out, then, check on Lady Bluebell."

The paper rustled as his dad turned the page. "No need, son. I've been out there. She's looking good. Breathing easier. More alert."

That his dad had done his chores for him was the last thing he wanted to hear. He'd been all ready to escape the house for a little while, kind of pull himself together after what had happened upstairs.

He *needed* some time on his own. "Good. But there are a few other things that want tending to. I won't be long."

The paper rustled again. "Suit yourself, son."

Belle, still aglow with what had happened upstairs, with the blinding realization she'd experienced right afterward, heard the door close as Preston went out. She picked up another potato and went to work with the peeler.

I love him. I love Preston McCade.

Every time she thought the words, they seemed more real to her. More true.

Charlotte said, "It's supposed to snow later tonight."

From behind his newspaper, Silas added, "Six to ten inches, maybe more. Says so right here."

Belle beamed down at the potato in her hand. Such a beautiful potato, such a fine, comfortable kitchen. And truly, Charlotte and Silas were two of the dearest people in the world. She could already smell the savory aroma of that rib roast in the oven. Doris had studded the meat with garlic and rubbed it with fragrant herbs. Out in the side yard, which she could see through the window over the sink, the snow had already started falling, great, white flakes of it gently drifting down.

It was going to be a lovely holiday evening.

And best of all, at the end of it, she would spend at least a few perfect hours in Preston's big, strong arms.

"It's already starting to get dark out there," Charlotte said.

Belle picked up another potato. "We should turn on the tree lights."

"We should indeed."

So Belle finished the potatoes and then went around the downstairs turning on the tree and the lights strung across the mantels. She even turned on the television to that channel that played holiday music. When she returned to the kitchen Michael Bublé was singing "It's Beginning to Look a Lot Like Christmas."

"Very festive." Charlotte nodded approvingly.

When Preston came back in, it was full dark outside—or it would have been if the yard hadn't blazed with thousands of Christmas lights. Belle was in the dining room by then setting the table. She heard the door close and knew that it had to be him. That lovely, fluttery feeling happened in her midsection. She paused in the act of adjusting a fork and listened for the sound of his footsteps on the stairs. Already, she knew his habits. When he came in from working, he would go straight upstairs to clean up.

But he must have left his boots outside. He went up without her hearing him.

A few minutes later, as she was filling the water glasses, he appeared in the archway to the living room. He wore a clean shirt and had Ben in his arms.

Their gazes met. Her heart turned over.

I love you, Preston. I love you. I do.

"Hi," he said softly. In his eyes, she saw it all. Everything. The night before. The wild and wicked magic they had shared just that afternoon.

"Hello."

"Belle, hi!" Ben did his own version of a wave, fisting his little hand, then spreading his fingers wide.

She gave the wave back to him in kind. "Hello, Benjamin."

He sighed and leaned his head on Preston's shoulder. "Dada…" He sounded dreamy. Content—his suffering of that afternoon forgotten, his bond with his father growing stronger by the day.

She said, "Dinner's almost ready."

Silas came in from the living room. "How about a little whiskey first?"

So they went into the living room. Silas offered drinks around. The McCade men had their whiskey. Ben had a sippy cup of watered-down apple juice. Belle and Charlotte each took a small amount of the Cabernet they would be enjoying with dinner.

Marcus appeared when they sat down to eat and the ranch hands came over from the cabin. Everyone agreed the food was first rate. They let Ben stay up for a while afterward because he'd had his nap so late. When he finally went to bed, Vince and Jack returned to their quarters. Preston, Silas and Marcus settled in to watch a poker tournament on television.

It was the perfect opportunity for Belle and Charlotte to get some presents wrapped. They worked until eleven. And when they were done, there was a nice, festive pile of packages underneath the big tree.

And Charlotte said, "I left a few things at Silas's house. I believe I'll walk across the yard with him, and bring them back to wrap."

A few minutes later, Marcus had retired to his room and Charlotte and Silas were on their way across the snowy yard. Belle and Preston were alone.

She got the baby monitor from the table in the living room and went into his arms at the foot of the stairs. "I've been thinking about that rocking horse up in the attic."

He brushed a tender finger along the side of her cheek. "Have you?" In his eyes were promises. The kind she could hardly wait for him to keep.

"I wonder if Richard Gibbons could repaint it, so it's all fresh and new."

"Ask him." He kissed her, just a light brush of his lips across hers.

"I believe I will," she said.

"I'll bring it down for you tomorrow."

"Perfect." They climbed the stairs together, their arms around each other.

She stayed in his bed until he got up to do his morning chores.

Back in her own room, she couldn't get back to sleep. So she showered and dressed and watched the dawn break from her bedroom window. The snow was white and endless to the far horizon, over a foot deep.

Doris showed up in her big four-wheel-drive pickup at nine on the dot.

There was more baking. Richard Gibbons came by in

the afternoon to take the rocking horse away. He said he would have it done by the end of the week.

Mary Beth Deluca called. She wondered if perhaps Belle and Charlotte would like to help out with the interdenomination holiday food and clothing drive.

Belle and Charlotte agreed that they would love to do whatever they could. So Belle told Mary Beth they would be available both Thursday and Friday to pick up donations and take what they gathered to the Masonic Hall, where everything would be packed up to be distributed to families in need.

That evening was like the one before it. Charlotte found another reason to go home with Silas. And Belle spent the night in Preston's bed.

The next morning, Tuesday, at a little after eight, a FedEx truck pulled into the yard. Belle knew what it was before the driver knocked on the door: the official paternity test results had arrived.

She signed for them but didn't open them. She would wait until Preston came in from working with the horses and feeding his cattle. She knew what the results would be, of course. But still, she felt a certain anticipation, a rising sensation in her chest. It was a big thing: the legal proof that Preston was Ben's father.

When he came in at two, she waited until he'd gone upstairs to shower. Then she got the cardboard envelope and went up to his room.

She tapped on his door, but he didn't answer. He was probably still in the shower. She tapped again, called his name—not too loudly. Ben was asleep the next door down. She tried the doorknob. It turned. He hadn't locked it, so she dared to go on in.

She was sitting on his bed when he emerged from the bath, freshly shaved, wearing nothing but a big white towel, carrying a second towel in his hand. The sight of him had her breath catching in her chest. She loved everything about him—the fine, clean, strong muscles of his arms, the shape of his lean feet, his thick, conservatively cut dark blond hair that was sticking straight up as he rubbed it with that second towel.

"Keep looking at me that way," he suggested low. "You'll force me to kiss you. And you know what will happen after that."

She sighed and almost told him that she loved him.

But no, it wasn't the time for that.

Not yet.

Instead, she brought the FedEx envelope out from behind her back and held it out to him. "It came this morning."

His big arms dropped to his sides and he said in a near-whisper, "The results…"

Nodding, she rose. "I thought you should be the one to open them."

He tossed the towel across a chair, held out his hand. She passed him the envelope. He stared silently down at it for several seconds. And then he looked up at her. "I keep thinking, what if…"

She understood his fear, but she had no doubt it was totally unfounded. "It's only the proof, Preston. We all know the truth."

Still, he didn't open the thing. He turned stiffly, went to the chair where he'd thrown the towel and sat down. "It's crazy. But I keep thinking…how I really don't remember what happened that night, between me and Anne. That seems a like a crime somehow. I…" His voice caught. He gulped. "He's mine, right? Nothing can change that." He held the envelope between his two hands, his big, broad shoulders slumped, and he looked up at her pleadingly, needing confirmation.

She gave it. "You're a fine man, Preston. You don't need to be so hard on yourself. Anne knew that you are Ben's father. If she'd had any doubts, she would have shared them at the end."

He swallowed hard again. And then he turned the envelope over and pulled the tab. He removed the results.

And stared down at them.

"Well?" she prompted, her heart suddenly racing. "What does it say?"

It took him what seemed like forever to look up at her again.

Finally, he did. "It's says there's a 99.9942% chance that I'm Ben's father." He looked absolutely terrified. "That's good, right? He's mine?"

She laughed. "Oh, Preston. Yes. In terms of statistical probabilities, that is as good as it gets. Ben is yours—which we already knew. You can stop worrying now."

He was blinking like someone had shined a blinding light in his eyes. "I knew it. But still, I can hardly believe it."

"Believe it." All at once, tears clogged her throat and burned her eyes. She thought of Anne, the summer before their junior year at Duke, standing on the pebbled shore at Rive Blanche, Montedoro's most famous beach, not far from the casino at Colline d'Ambre. Anne, in a white tank suit, her hands on her lean hips, staring out over the sea. Belle had called to her. She'd looked back over her shoulder with a tiny, faraway smile....

Anne. Gone. Lost to me forever. She pressed her lips together to keep them from trembling.

He saw. "What?" He swept to his feet. "Belle..." He reached for her.

With a sigh, she curved into him, into his warm, strong

arms. She rested her head against his bare chest. He smelled of soap and shaving cream.

He kissed her hair. "What is it? Tell me."

"It's Anne." She sighed and pressed her lips to the warm flesh of his shoulder. "I miss her. I'm going along fine and then…I don't know. It just comes at me all over again. It overwhelms me. The fact that she's gone. That I will never see her again in this life."

The test paper rustled as he gathered her closer. He didn't say anything. He just held her—until she straightened her spine and gently pulled free of his embrace.

She brushed the unwelcome tears from her eyes. "I'm sorry. It's a great moment. We should be celebrating."

He dropped the test results and the empty envelope on the chair and grasped her shoulders. "Don't be sorry. You lost your friend."

She tried to look away, but he only waited until she finally met his gaze again. "Really." She tried her best to sound reassuring. "I'm all right."

He wasn't convinced. "No. It's tough for you. I see that. Anne is…gone. And now, in a few weeks, you'll be saying goodbye to Ben."

Saying goodbye to Ben. Her heart seemed to drop to her midsection.

Because he said it so calmly. So surely. As though it had never even occurred to him that she might stay on, that the two of them might be sharing more than a holiday fling.

"But I thought that…" The dangerous words were almost out before she remembered to hold them back.

He held her gaze, blue eyes full of tender concern. "What? You thought what?"

She was jumping too fast, she knew that. Assuming too much. She needed to back off a little, give them both the time and the room they needed to see if they really might have some kind of a future together.

"Nothing," she said. "It's not important. Not now."

"*What's* not important?" he demanded.

She stared in his eyes and knew she was going to open her mouth and reveal the truth.

Chapter Twelve

But she didn't. Belle composed her expression. She went on tiptoe and kissed him. And she spoke gently, without heat. "Forgive me. It's an emotional time. I'm sad to have lost my friend. But I'm happy for you and for Ben."

Frowning, he studied her face. It took him several seconds to decide to believe that there was nothing bothering her beyond how much she missed Anne.

But in the end, he did believe it. He pulled her closer. "Thank you. For everything. For…more than I can ever repay."

The dangerous moment was over. She told herself she was glad. And she kissed him again and said he should hurry and get dressed, so they could share the big news.

And then Ben woke from his nap and she went to get him up and the rest of the day unfolded, all warm and cozy in the big, festively decorated ranch house.

Rhiannon called that evening. Belle took her phone upstairs for privacy while she talked to her sister.

"Did you think about what I told you?" Rhia asked.

"I did."

"And?"

"And then Saturday night, I seduced him."

Rhia laughed out loud. "Fabulous. And now?"

"It's beautiful here, snowy. The house is all done up for the holidays. Ben and Preston are growing closer." There were the tears again, rising, making her throat clutch. "And I think I'm falling in love."

Rhia gasped. "Oh, I knew it."

"Rhia, I want to tell him, to talk to him about the way I feel for him."

"So, then, you should talk to him."

"It seems too soon."

"Then wait."

Belle laughed through her tears. "You're no help."

Her sister said gently, "No. I suppose I'm not. But I love you and whatever you decide, I just know it will be the right thing."

"I just have this feeling, Rhia. That when I do tell him how much I care, he won't believe me. He won't believe that what we have is something that can last. He'll send me home. I don't know what to do. I truly don't."

"Then I will tell you. Slow down. Take a deep breath. And enjoy every minute."

Belle did her best to take her sister's advice. She kept busy for the rest of the day. And that night she spent, joyfully, in Preston's bed.

Wednesday morning, she got a call from the North Carolina investigator who had done the background check on Preston. Before he had time to do much but say his name, she told him that she'd satisfied herself as to Preston's suitability as a father and she would appreciate if he would send her a bill.

He laughed good-naturedly and told her that from his research, "Preston McCade is a real upstanding citizen. His ranch is in the black, he's never been arrested. Never been married. Nobody's suing him. Ran a red light once. But that's about the extent of his reprehensible behaviors. If you want more, I would need your go-ahead—along with my daily rate plus expenses—to take a trip to Montana and get a little more up close and personal on the man."

"That won't be necessary. Send me the bill?"

"You got it, Yer Highness. You take care now."

After she hung up, she went ahead and called Anne's attorney in Raleigh. She said she was preparing to turn custody of Ben over to his biological father. The attorney, who had been given previous instructions and a thorough briefing on the situation and possible outcomes, said he would have all the necessary documents overnighted to her that day. They could take them to Preston's attorney and proceed from there.

That night in bed, she told Preston that the private investigator she'd hired before she met him had called him an upstanding citizen. "I told him to send me the bill."

He laughed and nuzzled her neck. "He didn't mention all those banks I robbed?"

She moved in closer, rubbed her cheek against his scratchy one. "Everyone makes a mistake now and then." He cradled her breast, caught the nipple between his fingers and rolled it a little. "Don't distract me," she said a little breathlessly. "There's more."

He nibbled on her earlobe. "I'm listening."

"Tomorrow, we'll be getting a big pouch of documents from Anne's lawyer."

He was really listening now. He braced up on an elbow. In the light from the bedside lamp, his square-jawed, beard-scruffy face was eager, intent. "This is about my getting custody?"

She nodded. "Also, there's a large trust. Anne was quite well-off. Almost everything went to Ben. So you'll have to be brought up to speed on that."

"All right."

"You'll need a good lawyer on this end."

"I know one, Joshua Cawley. He does family law and estate planning. We've used him a couple of times and his work is always first rate. He's in Missoula."

"Do you think he could meet with us tomorrow? We should go right ahead with it, I think. Next week is Christmas week. It will be hard to get much done then...." And after that, it would be the New Year. She had a couple of speaking engagements in late January, for Nurses Without Boundaries. Her life...her *real* life...was calling her, rushing to meet her. This beautiful holiday season would be ending soon.

Way too soon.

Preston said, "I'll call him first thing. See if he can fit us in before the weekend."

"Wonderful. I told Mary Beth Deluca that Charlotte and I would help with the food and clothing drive tomorrow and Friday. But I'm sure she'll understand if I have to change plans. We could help Saturday, if she could use us then."

"Just as long as you save Saturday night for me."

Her heart lifted. "I just might do that. What, exactly, are you planning?"

"There's a dance at the Masonic Hall. Come with me." When he looked at her like that, she was absolutely certain there was no way he could let her go.

"I will consider it," she told him coolly. But then he

peeled back the blanket and touched her. A moment later, the only word on her lips was "Yes."

The papers from Anne's lawyer arrived first thing the next morning. Preston called his lawyer, who told him what personal documents he would need to bring. The attorney said he could see them that afternoon. That meeting took three hours. When Belle and Preston left Cawley's office, the transfer of custody was officially set in motion. There would be a hearing before a judge sometime in the New Year, Cawley had told them.

But it was only a formality because all the papers were in order, the child's guardian, Belle, would not contest the action and Ben's mother had made it clear in her will that Preston was her son's father and should be awarded custody if he so desired.

Friday morning, Richard Gibbons delivered the old rocking horse. He'd done a beautiful job restoring it to its former glory. Belle put it in the foyer by the tree, where they all could admire it. After the holidays, Preston could put it away, save it for when Ben was old enough to ride it.

Friday afternoon and Saturday morning, too, Belle and Charlotte and Marcus gathered clothes and food for families in need. Preston and Silas were left at the ranch with Ben. It was good practice, everyone agreed, for the McCade men to take care of the youngest McCade on their own.

Mary Beth and the other ladies who ran the drive were grateful for the help. When Mary Beth learned of Belle's work, she said how important it was "To get out into the world and lend a helping hand…and you know, Belle, if you ever considered moving to Montana, we could keep you real busy. We're always looking for team leaders and coordinators for the state's Red Cross efforts. And then we have our United Way donation drives and any number of worthy projects run by the members of our local churches."

Belle was touched. "I certainly have felt welcome here. And I do appreciate your hospitality."

Mary Beth blushed and allowed as how she'd never known a real princess before. "It's an honor, I must tell you. Especially given that you are as lovely inside as out."

Belle wanted to cry again. It was getting ridiculous. She'd always been a bit sentimental, but not the sort who burst into tears just because someone kind said something nice to her. She thanked Mary Beth and then got back into the SUV where Marcus waited so patiently behind the wheel.

They left to make another round of donation pickups.

Saturday, they worked into the afternoon. The weather was clear that day and icy-cold. No new snow was predicted for the rest of that pre-Christmas weekend.

That night, Charlotte and Silas had volunteered to stay home and take care of Ben so that Belle and Preston could attend the Christmas dance at the Masonic Hall. Belle spent a lot of time up in her room getting ready. Because the weather would be clear, she felt reasonably safe wearing the most festive outfit she'd brought with her: a slim, knee-length red velvet skirt and a close-fitting short red jacket with a V neck and three-quarter-length sleeves. She had a lovely pair of hose with a back seam and a tiny red poinsettia flower woven at the base of the seam, just above her ankles. And her best red high heels. She swept her hair up into a twist and wore diamond studs in her ears.

She'd packed the festive ensemble in a gesture of defiance way back at the end of October, when she flew to North Carolina to take care of Anne. Then, she'd still had some hope that Anne might last through Christmas. Pack-

ing the bright skirt and jacket had made the possibility of
Anne's living longer seem more real somehow.

Yes, she knew that the shoes were a little dangerous on
icy Elk Creek streets, but she would hold on to Preston's
arm nice and tight for stability.

When she came down the stairs and joined the others
in the living room, Silas whistled and Charlotte said, "You
look absolutely beautiful, dearest."

Preston, so handsome in black trousers and a dressy
black shirt, said softly, "Oh, yeah, she does."

They had the Christmas music playing and the big tree
all lit up. Ben sat on the rug trying to stack bright-colored
foam blocks. At the sight of Belle, he cried, "Belle! Play!"

And Preston bent to scoop him up into his big arms.
"Belle is all ready for the night out with me, bud. She's not
getting down on the rug with you right now. But I'm thinking she might be willing to give us a dance."

Ben called her name again and held out his arms. Her
heart overflowing with love and tenderness so sharp it was
almost painful, she went to them.

A new song started, "I'll Be Home for Christmas." They
danced, Preston and Belle, with Ben between them. They
swayed in time to the bittersweet song, into the foyer, in
front of the tree.

Ben made soft happy sounds, alternately leaning his
head on Preston's shoulder and then on Belle's. A bright
light went off, surprising Belle so that she laughed.

Preston said, "Back off, Dad." Silas had gone and gotten a camera. And he didn't listen to Preston. He snapped
a couple more quick shots as they danced.

When the song was over, Ben clung to Belle. She took
him and went into the living room and sat on the sofa. The
others joined her. For a while they sat and chatted, Ben
quiet in her lap, his head on her shoulder, relaxed in her

arms. She savored those moments, her heart full and aching at the same time.

Preston had a reservation at The Bull's Eye for dinner before the dance. She sat across from him at the same table he'd reserved the night they met and couldn't help fantasizing what it might be like if she did stay with him, if they made a life together. The Bull's Eye might become "their" special place. She loved that idea.

"You're smiling," he said, quietly. Intimately. "It's your secret smile. What goes through your mind when you smile like that?"

It was a good opening. She shocked herself and took it. "I was thinking about us, about how things might be if we stayed together. That we might come here often. It could be 'our place.'"

He gazed at her steadily when she said that, his eyes unreadable. And then he picked up the whiskey he'd ordered and knocked back a big gulp of it. "Sometimes it's better not to go imagining things that aren't going to happen."

That hurt. And she couldn't quite just let it go. "How do you know it won't happen? How do you know you won't... want to be with me longer than just until New Year's?"

He glanced away. His hand on the table had formed a fist. "Come on, Belle. Don't."

She pushed on, lowering her voice another notch, keeping it carefully controlled. "Answer my question. Please."

"Not here."

"Then where? When?"

He kept trying not to look at her. But she stared straight at him until, at last, he met her eyes. "It's not about what I want. Sometimes a guy doesn't get what he wants."

She leaned closer. "You have to know that makes no sense at all. If you want to be with me and I want to be with you, well, then, we just…do what we have to do to make that happen."

His face was so…tight. Closed off from her. "Can we please not talk about this now?"

Oh, she did long to keep pushing. Somehow, now she'd finally opened her mouth and tried to say what was on her mind and in her heart, she just didn't want to stop. They needed to speak of this. Or at least, *she* needed to.

But he did have a point. Perhaps now, in The Bull's Eye before the big Christmas dance, was not the right time to do it.

"All right, Preston." She picked up her fork and ate a bite of her potato. "We'll discuss it later."

Pres could already tell that the evening was pretty much ruined.

He picked up his fork and knife and went to work on his porterhouse. Across from him, Belle was way too silent. She ate her meal methodically, so beautiful it hurt to look at her in that perfectly fitted red velvet jacket, diamonds sparkling in her delicate ears.

He tried to think of something neutral to say, but then that seemed pretty damn fake to pretend that nothing had happened.

Yeah, okay. It was a conversation they apparently needed to have. He had to make it clear to her that there was this time they were having, so fine and perfect, like a dream come true.

And there was real life. He wasn't moving to some European country to hang out with the jet set. And damned if he would ask her—or even *let* her—give up what was hers by rights, a life of glamour and privilege, to move to Montana and be a ranch wife.

They finished the meal in a strained, unhappy silence.

When they left The Bull's Eye, he almost asked her if she wanted to just head back to the ranch. But she hadn't said a word about cutting the evening short—she hadn't said much of anything since he'd asked her to stop talking about their nonexistent future together.

Maybe, once they got to the dance, once he got his arms around her on the dance floor, the mood would lighten up a little. They could put the heavy issues aside. They could do what he'd assumed they had agreed to be doing together: enjoying a beautiful time while it lasted.

The Masonic Hall was all done up for the party, with a Christmas tree in every corner and lights strung from the rafters. They checked their coats and went in. A five-piece band, the one the Community Club always got for town dances, was playing "Let It Snow."

Pres took Belle's hand and led her over to the punch table. He poured them each a paper cupful. She took hers with a nod, her lips moving, saying "Thank you," though he didn't hear the words. The band was too loud.

They stood there, sipping the too-sweet punch, waving occasionally to people they knew as the music grated in his ears. He felt grim and determined and realized he'd hardly felt grim at all since Belle had brought Ben and Charlotte and the damn bodyguard and moved into his house.

And then he started thinking how he used to feel that way all the time, how being with Belle kind of put a whole new light on every day, and brightened every night. How he'd been losing himself in just being with her and not let himself think about how it was going to be when she left.

Yeah, at least he'd have Ben. That mattered a lot. Ben would give him a focus and a hope in his life that he'd lost somewhere along the way.

But it was still going to be pretty damn awful to wake up every day and not once see her smile across a table at him, not once hear that voice of hers that was cultured and musical and sexy as hell. Not be able to turn to her for advice about Ben. Not be able to ask her opinion when he was considering the pros and cons of just about anything.

Not to have her with him in his bed. For the lovemaking, which with her was the best he'd ever had—and yeah, it wasn't like he had a lot to compare it to. But still. A man knows the best when he's having it. And with Belle, it was the best, bar none.

And what about the simple feel of her skin, the way she sighed in her sleep, the smell of her hair?

How was he supposed to get by without the smell of her hair?

And why the hell did she have to bring this up and get him so he couldn't stop thinking about it anyway?

"Let It Snow" finally ended. The band launched into something slow and sweet.

He turned to her and took the half-empty cup of punch from her. He set the cup on the refreshment table and put his cup beside it. "Let's dance."

She went into his arms. The world filled up with her: with the scent of her subtle, tempting perfume, the feel of her soft, smooth body under the red velvet she wore. He closed his eyes and pretended that right now, this moment, was all that there was. Just him and Belle, dancing together to an old Willie Nelson song his mom used to play at Christmastime before they lost her.

He tried to hold on to that feeling, the feeling of him and Belle together, right now. The feeling that the past and the future didn't matter, didn't even exist.

When the song ended, she smiled at him.

He took that to mean the rough patch was over. They could go ahead as they had been. Through the holidays.

Until the New Year.

They danced some more. When the band took a break, she left him to visit the ladies' room. He stood by the refreshment table and talked horses with Gil Belquist, who owned the Triple B Ranch, southwest of town.

Gil turned to get more punch. He bent over the table and past his shoulders Pres caught sight of Lucy, standing by the door. Staring at him.

What was her problem, anyway?

But then Belle returned and the band started playing again. He took her in his arms and there was only the two of them. The way it ought to be for every last second of the time they had left together.

They were quiet on the ride home, but it seemed to him a comfortable kind of silence. He was really thinking that things were okay between them again.

Inside, Charlotte and the old man were waiting up. They reported that Ben had been a little angel. He'd gone to bed without a fuss.

Then Charlotte said, "I'll just walk Silas across the yard...."

They put on their coats and left.

Pres turned to Belle—and he knew as soon as he looked in her eyes. Things were not okay. In the restaurant, she'd said they could discuss it later.

Later was now.

"Let's go in the living room," she said.

He trudged in after her, feeling like a condemned man on the way to the execution chamber. She waited until he was inside, then she shut the wide doors to the foyer and checked the baby monitor that Charlotte had left on the coffee table, making sure it was on.

She sat on the sofa. He took the seat across from her. It seemed wrong, somehow, to sit next to her for this.

"Please, Preston." She leaned forward, toward him, her

hands tightly folded in her lap. "I only want you to know that I…I care for you. I care for you deeply. And I have been thinking that I don't want it to end with us. I don't want us to just walk away from each other once the holidays are over. I want…well, I want more. More time with you. More *life* with you."

God, she was beautiful. It wasn't fair how beautiful she was. He never should have gotten anything started with her. He could see that now. Now, he was the one stuck trying to make her see reason. "I'm crazy about you, Belle. You know that."

Her face seemed to light from within. "Well, all right, then. What is the problem? I'm not asking you to marry me." She blushed in the prettiest way. "Not yet anyway. I'm only saying that if we both want to be together, why don't we just…allow for the possibility that there might be more for us beyond the New Year?"

"What more? I'm not moving to Montedoro, Belle. I belong here. My life is here."

"I know that." She said it so simply. Calmly.

He put up both hands. "Hold on. Wait a minute. You're actually considering…I mean, you have some idea that *you* might move *here,* to Elk Creek?"

"I do, yes. I am considering a move to Elk Creek."

"Belle, that's beyond crazy. That's just purely insane."

She sat back from him then. Her eyes turned guarded. "It certainly is not. I think I could fit in here."

"It's not a question of your fitting in. You'd be bored out of your skull inside of a month."

"Excuse me." Now the color in her face was more of the pissed-off variety. "Have I seemed *bored* to you?"

"Belle, you've been here two weeks. It's the holidays. Wait till mid-February. You won't be able to get out of Montana fast enough."

She sat up even straighter. "I think you're wrong."

"You haven't lived through a Montana winter yet."

"But I could, no problem. I am a person with resources, Preston. And I'm not talking about money. I have a rich internal life. I know how to keep myself occupied with productive activities. I love to read and to study. I've already spoken with Mary Beth Deluca about the various community projects with which I might become involved were I to make my home here. I could still travel for my work. And I would also be interested in helping you with the horses. It so happens I love horses. And then there would be Ben. I would be spending a lot of time with him."

It all came clear to him then. "Ben." He said it gently.

"Yes. Of course. Ben." She frowned. "Why are you looking at me like that?"

"Well, because I get it now. It's about Ben."

She put her hand to her throat. "About Ben? I don't understand."

He laid it right out on the table. "If you stay here, you don't have to give him up."

She lowered that hand back to her lap and then she just sat there, looking at him for several seconds that seemed like forever. When she did speak, each word was ice-cold. "I've been prepared to give Ben up from the first. That's why I came here, in case you don't remember."

"I know. But if you hook up with me, you won't have to."

She smiled. It was not a happy expression. "I'm very tempted to say something sarcastic and heavy with irony right now. But instead, I'll simply tell you directly that yes, it would be wonderful for me to be here to help Ben grow up. I would give a lot for the chance at that. But Ben doesn't need *me* to grow up strong and capable. He will have you and Silas to guide him. And this excellent community you have here in Elk Creek. So there's simply no need for me to sacrifice my own life to see that he is well cared for. If I chose to live here, to remain here, with you, it would be for *you,* Preston. For you and for me and for what we might share together."

By God, he was starting to believe her. And that scared the hell out of him. He stood up. "I…I can't, Belle. Since we started, I've hated even thinking about how it will be when you go. Now you're telling me you're thinking that maybe you *won't* go. And all I can think is… You say that now. When it's all exciting and new and fresh between us. But what will you say in a month? In a year? If I had you for a year, and *then* you left me…" His throat locked up. He swallowed, hard. "I can't do that. I think it would kill me."

She rose, too, regal as any queen. "Your mother died, you know? She didn't *leave* you."

"What?" He let his annoyance with that train of thought show. "You're going to start psychoanalyzing me now?"

"No, I'm only pointing out that you lost your mom at a tender age. And you never really tried with a woman until Lucy. And we know that did not go well. It could be you're so reluctant to give this thing between us a chance because experience has taught you that you'll only be disappointed."

"Maybe experience has taught me right."

"If men never took a chance on women, Preston, the human race would be doomed."

Why couldn't he make her understand? "Belle, I can't, okay? I just can't."

"That's not so. You can. You simply won't. Do you see me as a flighty sort of person? Someone who makes commitments and then changes her mind about them?"

"No. Never. You're not like that. That's not what I mean. It's only…" He didn't know how to finish. So he just stood there, feeling awkward and awful and out of his depth.

She came around the table toward him and didn't stop

until she stood right in front of him. His arms ached to reach for her, to pull her close, crush his mouth down on hers.

To forget all this talk of what might be. To lose himself in the moment, in the shine of the firelight on her hair, in the scent of her skin, the softness of her body pressed good and close to his....

But he didn't reach for her. He kept his hands hard at his side.

She was the one who reached out. She lifted her slim, smooth hand and pressed her palm to his cheek. He felt that touch so deep inside, in places no one had ever touched him before. She said, "My sister Rhia told me that I ought to take a chance on you."

He answered in a low rumble. "She doesn't even know me."

"No, but she knows *me*. She knows I can be...cautious. That I could be one of those people who won't risk loving for fear of a broken heart."

"There's nothing wrong with a little caution."

"No." She took her hand away. It needed every ounce of will he possessed not to grab it back. "But sometimes one has to be bolder, to risk getting hurt, to find the kind of love that lasts a lifetime—or so my sister said." She turned and walked away from him. He watched her go, aching so bad to call her back, but knowing she wanted more from him than he was brave enough to give. At the doors, she paused and faced him again. "I'll leave the monitor here. If Ben needs you in the night, I know you'll be there for him. In the morning, when you go out to the stables, just open my bedroom door and put the monitor inside. I'll take it from there."

And that was all. She opened the doors and went through, leaving him behind.

Chapter Thirteen

Everything was the same.

And yet it was all completely changed.

Pres went to bed alone. And in the morning before dawn, when he got up to go out to the stables, he left an empty room behind. He slipped the baby monitor inside her door, just like she'd asked him to.

Temptation was a real bitch. He couldn't stop himself. He opened the door wider than he needed to. And for a minute—or maybe three—he stood there, staring into her darkened bedroom, breathing the air she breathed, staring at the shape of her across the room, under the covers, dimly seen through the gloom.

Then, very quietly, he pulled that door closed.

At nine, they went to Mass. And then into town for lunch at the diner. Belle was gracious and gentle as always. She smiled at him more than once. But it wasn't the same kind of smile she would have given him the day before.

It wasn't an intimate smile.

At home, Charlotte set to work making her family recipe for chicken with wine. She said, "Silas can help me and we can take care of Ben. Why don't you two go outside? Perhaps a horseback ride? Belle loves to ride."

He waited for Belle to speak up and say how she didn't feel like a ride right now, how she didn't want to go outside—especially not with him.

But then she only gave him one of those new cordial-but-not-intimate smiles. "Would you mind, Preston? I would love to go riding."

He kind of wondered what she was up to, but what could he say? "Sure. Weather's clear for once. We can ride."

"Thank you. I'll just tell Marcus where I'm going so he won't worry...."

The bodyguard came along, although he rode behind them, far enough back that it was easy to pretend he wasn't even there.

Belle wore tan riding breeches and English riding boots. But she took right to the Western saddle. And she had a fine, easy seat on a horse. They took some trails he knew where the snow tended to pile up off the riding path. It was pretty easy going, a lot of it under the tall, sheltering branches of the evergreens.

She didn't talk much. But then, neither did he. Mostly, he was wondering if maybe she was rethinking sleeping separate from him. If maybe she was deciding that she wouldn't mind enjoying the rest of the time they could have together, kind of going back to their old understanding of how it would be.

He told himself how that wouldn't be a good idea, how if she did have some notion that they could be temporary lovers after all, he would just tell her he didn't see how that could work. That it was just asking for a big old heap of trouble. That she had been right to go to her room alone last night.

But who did he think he was kidding?

All she had to do was crook her little finger. He'd have her buck naked with those fine, slim legs in the air lickety-split—the watchful bodyguard be damned.

Once a cottontail rabbit ran across their path. The horses shied. She laughed and had the frisky white mare he'd given her settled and easy in about a second flat.

So, yeah, she knew horses. And she knew how to handle them. He'd figured as much from those things she said about her sister Alice that first night, about the Akhal-Tekes they kept in Montedoro. But it was one thing to know it in his head and another to ride out at her side and be confident she knew what she was doing.

Back at the stables, he told her to go on inside, he'd take care of the horses. But she insisted she could unsaddle her own horse. And she did, removing the bridle first, then taking his tips on how to proceed, given the differences between the Western saddle and the English saddle she was accustomed to.

Once the horses were groomed and free in the near paddock, she thanked him. And then she turned and left him standing there, staring after her gorgeous swaying backside, wishing he had grabbed her and kissed her and promised her anything if she would only be with him again.

He slept alone that night.

It was bad. He'd known that it would be. That he would suffer like hell when she left him.

He just hadn't expected to do all this suffering when she was still right there in the house with him. She and Charlotte and Marcus spent most of the next day in Missoula, finishing up the Christmas shopping. And then, when they came home, the old man took off. He said he had some Christmas shopping of his own to do. He didn't get home until after dinner, but Charlotte had kept a plate ready for him.

She fussed over him, getting him a glass of whiskey, jumping up to get him more bread. He actually kissed her when she passed him the butter. You'd think they were newlyweds sometimes, the way the two of them carried on. It annoyed Pres no end. Didn't the old man have any clue how tough it was going to be for him when Charlotte left with Belle?

Apparently not. His dad seemed to be much better than he was at living in the moment, at enjoying a good thing while he had it and not worrying about the pain that was coming down the pike.

That evening, Belle reminded him that he needed to start thinking about hiring a nanny, someone to take care of Ben when he and the old man were out working.

He said, "Yeah, I'll get right on it."

"When?" she asked so sweetly.

"The day after Christmas. How's that?"

"That will be fine. Would you like me to ask Mary Beth or Father Francis if they have anyone they would recommend?"

"Thanks, but I can handle it."

She didn't say anything after that. Only nodded.

And walked away.

Another lonely night dragged by.

And all of a sudden, it was Christmas Eve. The women played Christmas music all day. He was getting pretty tired of hearing "White Christmas." But then, his nerves were generally shot.

Every night Belle wasn't with him was a whole new kind of purgatory.

And he knew she was leaving right after New Year's.

That meant a week of constant suffering, wanting to talk to her the way they used to talk, with warmth and understanding between them. Wanting to touch her when touching was not allowed. Yeah. Another week of that.

Then she would go.

And he would probably be even more miserable than he was now.

It was getting so he couldn't remember why he'd turned her down Saturday night—well, okay. He did know. It was so he wouldn't suffer in a year or two when she realized she was sick and tired of being a rancher's wife and decided to hightail it back to her villa by the sea in glittering, glamorous Montedoro. It was because it was going to be so damn much worse to lose her later than to go ahead and bite the bullet now.

God in heaven. He didn't see how it could get all that much worse than this.

Over dinner that night, they discussed attending Midnight Mass and the candlelight service. But they decided to skip it that year.

"Next year," his dad promised, sharing a rather intimate look with Charlotte. "No matter what."

"No matter what," Charlotte answered softly.

After Ben was in bed and Marcus had retired to his room, the old man appeared in the family room with a bottle of champagne in one hand and four fluted crystal glasses between the gnarled fingers of the other. He raised the bottle high. "Let's pop this champagne. Shar and I have an announcement to make."

At which point Charlotte, on the sofa, jumped to her feet. "Silas." She gave him a look. One of those looks that women have been giving men since the dawn of time. "We discussed this."

The old man blustered back, "I'm an impatient man,

Shar. I'm tired of waitin'. It's time we laid it on out there, time everyone knew our plans."

She hustled to his side, grabbed his arm and spoke in a flustered whisper. "There are others to consider here and you know that."

He dipped his gray head and planted a kiss on her up-turned mouth.

"Silas!" She was blushing.

"Then you better damn well consider 'em now. I am poppin' this cork tonight, one way or another."

"Oh, Silas…"

He bent close and kissed her again. "Go on, now," he said, his mustache twitching with his devilish smile and his voice downright tender. "Do what you need to do…."

Charlotte sighed. And then she nodded. And then she let go of his arm and turned to Belle, who was watching them with an expression that fell midway between be-mused and slightly stunned. "I wonder if we might share a private word?"

Belle got up. She raised her head high and put on a gentle smile, the way she always did when she faced something difficult. For a moment, Pres forgot all about his own suffering and only wanted to get his arms around her and tell her it was going to be okay—even if it wasn't. Everyone knew what was happening here. Ben wasn't the only one Belle would be leaving behind come the New Year. "Of course," she said, still smiling. "Let's go upstairs."

Belle shut the door of her bedroom and went to sit on the side of the bed beside her longtime companion.

Charlotte had her hands folded in her lap—but she couldn't keep them still. From folding them she had quickly progressed to wringing them.

Belle put her hand over both of Charlotte's. "Come now.

It's not as terrible as all that. In fact, if I've assumed correctly, it seems that something wonderful has happened and congratulations are in order."

Charlotte's hands stilled—but her shoulders dropped. "I've been trying since Sunday to find a way to tell you. But I know that things aren't going well with you and Preston. I didn't want to…make things worse. I hate to leave you. I…" She blew out a heavy breath in lieu of saying the rest.

It did hurt. To think of losing Charlotte, too. It hurt a great deal. But it was also cause for real rejoicing. Belle did her best to focus on the joy. "So, then, you're marrying Silas and staying here?"

Charlotte sniffled and swallowed hard. "It's horrible of me, I know."

Belle squeezed Charlotte's hands and then put her arm around her friend. She guided Charlotte's head down on her shoulder. "Listen. Are you listening?"

Charlotte sniffled again. "Yes. Yes, I am."

"I am so happy for you. Silas is a lucky man—and he's also a wonderful man."

"He is. Yes." There was more sniffling.

Belle reached over, snagged a tissue from the box on the nightstand and passed it to Charlotte. "You have waited far too long to have your happiness."

"But what about *your* happiness, dearest?" A sob escaped Charlotte. She did her best to swallow it back. "Oh, I'm such a ninny."

"No, you most definitely are not a ninny." Belle stroked her silver-threaded light brown hair, breathed in the rose scent she always wore. "And as for my happiness, one day I shall have it. Just you watch. But for now, I'm very happy that my dearest friend has found what she's been looking for. And think how perfect this is for our Ben. We've been so worried that he won't have enough of a woman's influence in his life as he grows. But now we know that he will. He will have his beloved Shar-Shar right there with him, to love him and care for him, every single day from this day forward. And we won't have to worry about finding the right nanny in a big hurry. You can take care of that in time as you see fit."

Charlotte sniffed again. And then she lifted her head from Belle's shoulder. "This tissue is hopelessly soggy. Could you pass me another?"

Belle did just that. "Now, I want you to dry your eyes and we'll go downstairs and toast to the coming union of two of my favorite people in this whole, wide world."

So they went down to join the men. Silas opened the champagne and they toasted the engagement of Preston's father and Charlotte. Belle took care not to glance in Preston's direction during the toasts. She didn't know what she might do or say if she caught him looking her way.

She was absolutely livid with him for turning his back on what they might have shared together. She was furious and she was deeply hurt. She would have hated him.

If only she didn't love him so much.

The few hours until bedtime dragged by. But finally, at ten, she allowed herself to say good-night. Upstairs in the bathroom she went through the motions, cleansing her face, brushing her teeth. Then she crossed the hall to her room, put on a plain white nightgown and got into bed. She heard Preston come up. It seemed to her he hesitated in front of her door.

Her heart stopped.

And then recommenced beating in a glum and plodding way when he went on by and entered his own room. She heard him close his door.

Two hours later, the Christmas lights in the yard had

gone out and she was still wide awake, lying there in the dark, staring up at the shadowed ceiling, wishing she dared to simply pack her things and leave in the morning.

But no. There was more than her broken heart to consider here. If she left early, Charlotte would know exactly how bad off she was. After all, Charlotte was well aware of how determined and focused she could be. If her pain was so great that she couldn't see this visit through until the New Year, well, Charlotte would worry. And she didn't want her loyal longtime companion worrying any more than absolutely necessary. Charlotte fully deserved the happiness she'd found. She deserved to have a glorious first holiday season with her newfound true love. And Belle was determined to see that she got it.

Plus, there was Ben. He was adjusting marvelously to his new life here in Montana, to his father and his grandfather. But another week with Belle available to him seemed wise. Yes, he needed to move on, to let her go. And she was working on that, shifting the responsibility for him more and more to Preston and Silas. And after tonight, she could add Charlotte into that mix. The goal was to have everyone *but* Belle caring for him by the time she left. With Charlotte to count on, pulling away from Ben was going to be a lot smoother than she would have dared to hope.

And that just made her feel more lost and alone and hopeless.

She considered getting up and calling home. Talking to Rhia might help.

But then again, no matter what she did now, it was going to be a hellish week. No need to drag her sister down into her misery with her.

Maybe a little hot milk would help soothe her, help her get a little sleep. She was pushing back the covers and lowering her feet to the rug when she heard the explosion outside—a horrible, screeching sound, followed by a crash and an ear-flaying crunching of metal.

A second later, it all happened again.

A horn started honking. And kept honking. One long, continuous wail of sound.

She let out a small cry of alarm and ran to the window. It took her startled brain several seconds to register what she saw.

In the light of the half moon, she saw that a red pickup had crashed into the big pine tree in the center of the yard. And then a black pickup had crashed into the red one. One headlight on each vehicle remained on, beaming bright streams of light into the frozen Montana night.

That horn kept honking.

As she whirled from the window to grab her robe, she saw the lights go on at Silas's house and the ranch hands' cabin—and heard Ben start crying. Swiftly, she pulled on her robe and put on her slippers.

Preston emerged from his room as she came out of hers. Even with the horn blaring and Ben yowling, they both stopped stock-still for a moment and stared at each other. The constant aching in her heart turned to agony.

Then Preston finished zipping up his jeans. "You get Ben? I'll go down."

"Yes, all right." She shook herself and turned for Ben's room.

Ben was inconsolable, standing in his crib, screaming for Anne.

Belle rushed to him and scooped him up. "Oh, Ben. It's all right. You're safe, my darling. Safe…"

He pushed at her and told her no and called out "Mama!" over and over.

She carried him to the rocker and sat down and rocked him until he stopped pushing her away and grabbed her close instead, until he stopped crying for Anne and sobbed her name. "Belle, Belle..."

"Yes, oh yes. That was so scary. I was scared, too. But you are safe and I have got you and everything is going to be all right...."

"Belle." He gave a soggy little sniff and nuzzled her neck. "Belle..."

Charlotte appeared in the open doorway to the upstairs hall, those big eyes wider than ever.

Belle stroked Ben's soft hair and cradled him close to her heart. "What happened?"

"Preston's old girlfriend had a fight with her husband."

"Lucy and Monty, you mean?"

Charlotte nodded. "She took off in her truck and he took off after her. Somehow, she ended up here. She crashed into the pine tree out in front. And *he* crashed into her."

"Insane."

"My thought exactly."

"Were they drinking?"

"Surprisingly, no. Just young and wildly in love and very, very stupid."

"Are they...all right?"

"She has a broken nose, I think. It appears that he's broken his leg and dislocated a shoulder."

"Oh, dear God..."

"We've called an ambulance. But I think you should come down and have a look at them. Here. I'll take Ben...."

Belle rose and handed him over. At first, he held on, his little arms tight around her neck. She feared he would make a fuss. But then he sighed, "Shar-Shar," and went to her willingly.

Belle went downstairs. They had brought the young couple inside to the family room. Monty lay on the sofa. Lucy, holding a bloody rag to her nose, knelt beside him.

Silas, Preston, Marcus and the two hands stood well back. All of them looked as though they would prefer to be anywhere but there.

Lucy was crying. "Oh, Monty. I love you. You know that I do."

Monty moaned. "Say it again."

"I love you. I do. I love you so much. But you're always so busy, you never have time for me."

"I love you, too. You gotta know that. And it's for us, Luce. I'm working for us, for our future, for you and for me and for the kids we're gonna have someday.... And why did you have to come *here?*" He sent a baleful glance in Preston's general direction. "Come lookin' for *him?*"

"Oh, don't you see?" Lucy took the rag away from her nose long enough to swipe at her eyes. "It's the only way I can get your attention, to try and make you jealous just a little...." She touched his shoulder.

He groaned in pain.

"Oh!" she cried. "Oh, my honey bear, I'm so sorry. Does it hurt so very much?"

"Say it again," he muttered low and with real passion.

"Honey bear, you're my honey bear. My own, sweet, handsome honey bear..."

Silas made a groaning sound. It had nothing to do with physical pain. When Belle glanced at him, he started making frantic gestures that she should step in and do a little nursing—and shut those two up while she was at it.

Belle cleared her throat. "Excuse me, I'm a nurse. I understand an ambulance has been called. But if you don't mind, I would like to have a quick look at both of you, just to be certain there's nothing that requires immediate attention."

Lucy's blond head whipped around. "Oh! You're the princess, right? How do you do, Your Royal Highness?"

"I am perfectly well, thank you. And please, call me Belle. Now let's have a look at your husband first, shall we?"

"Whatever you need to do, Your Majesty. Just ease his pain, ease my honey bear's terrible pain."

"I'll, er, do my best." She sent a glance toward the huddle of men. "Would one of you get some ice for Lucy's nose, please?"

"You got it." Silas headed for the kitchen.

Belle examined Monty. She had Preston help her immobilize his injured leg. For the shoulder, she warned Monty to keep it still and hoped the ambulance would be quick in coming. Dislocations were terribly painful, but he really should have X-rays before anyone attempted to put the bone back into the socket.

She was just turning to have a look at Lucy when they heard the ambulance siren approaching.

A half hour later, Lucy and Monty were off to the hospital in Missoula. Preston turned on the Christmas lights outside and Belle turned on the ones inside. Charlotte came downstairs and reported that Ben had gone back to sleep. They agreed it was a good sign that he'd recovered from the painful incident so quickly. Charlotte went to the kitchen to make hot chocolate. The men joined them at the kitchen table. They drank chocolate and ate big slices of Doris's cranberry-orange bread and waited for the tow trucks to arrive.

It was after three when the two wrecked vehicles were finally towed from the yard. The ranch hands said goodnight and went back to the cabin. In an hour or two, they would be up again, seeing to the horses and cattle and the chickens in the run out back. So would Preston. Ranch work never ended. Chores had to be done even on Christmas morning.

Marcus left them for his solitary room off the kitchen.

Charlotte and Silas said good-night. Their arms around each other, they turned for the house across the yard. Belle smiled to see them go. It was the first time Charlotte hadn't come up with some excuse for why she was going home with Preston's father.

Charlotte needed no excuse. Not anymore. She had found her love.

That left Preston and Belle standing alone on the shadowed front porch of the main house. He opened the door for her. She went in and turned off the inside Christmas lights and thought how she'd be turning them on again in just a few more hours, how she only wished she would be turning those lights on and off at Christmastime for the rest of her days.

But too often in life, a woman's dearest wish is not destined to come true.

She stood at the big window that looked out over the yard in front and watched the outside Christmas lights go dark as Preston turned them off. Her eyes adjusted quickly and she studied the old pine in the light of the moon. The trunk was newly scarred from the impact of Lucy's red pickup. But the tree still stood tall. It would probably be standing there for years to come.

"Belle."

It was Preston's voice from the doorway to the foyer behind her. So deep and strong, but tender, too. The sound sent a warm shiver through her. Hope rose anew.

He said, "Monty Polk is a stone idiot, but at least he's got the guts to tell his woman how he feels about her."

She turned to him then. "Oh, Preston…"

And then he said, "Belle, I can't take this anymore. I should be a bigger man. I should let you go. But if you still…" His voice caught. Her heart soared. "Anything, Belle," he said at last in a rough rumble. "I'll do anything if you'll only give me one more chance."

Chapter Fourteen

Inside, she was trembling.

But her outstretched hand was steady. "All you ever had to do was be willing to give the two of us a chance."

He came to her, his boots eating up the space between them in three long strides. He took her hand. As his rough fingers closed around hers, warmth suffused her. She knew the sweetest sensation. It was joy, pure and simple. He said, "It's all been so fast. In an instant. Do you realize it's been only three weeks since I walked into the Sweet Stop and found you sitting there?"

She gazed up at him. She would never grow tired of looking at him. Even in the dim light of the darkened room, his blue eyes were shining. "I knew you were someone special, Preston. From that very first moment."

"And I knew you were the most beautiful woman I'd ever seen. And also a million miles above me."

"No, that's not so—except maybe in your mind. Since

I met you, I've only wanted to stand beside you. And the way I remember it, you did ask me to dinner right then and there. Hardly the first move of a man who's decided he's beneath me."

He chuckled then, a somewhat baffled sound. "I don't know what got into me. I was thinking how I would never have a chance with you. And then, a second later, I was asking you out."

"And I was…in turmoil. I wanted to go out with you—for your own sake. And that was completely inappropriate. I needed to be thinking about how to tell you that Anne had died and left you a son."

"Come here," he commanded, rough and tender at once. "Come close.…"

"Oh, Preston." She swayed against him, wrapped her arms around his lean waist, tipped her face up to look at him. "I've been so angry at you. It's been horrible."

"Yeah." He put a finger under her chin, caressed her cheek. "I knew you were. But I was stuck on the idea that I was doing the right thing, that it could never work with us in the long run. That we were just…something perfect and magical and not meant to last, something beautiful that happened one holiday season. I had this idea that I should let you go now, for your sake, because you could do a lot better.…"

"That's not so."

He touched her lips with his thumb. "I don't know. Maybe it is."

"It's not."

"Well, it seemed so to me. And I also, well, I wanted to get losing you over with. I told myself that it would only be harder when you walked away later."

"Who said I would walk away later?"

"I just assumed. That you would grow tired of me, that you'd get bored living here."

"I thought we talked about that."

"Yeah. Well. I guess I wasn't listening."

Remembering the pain of that night made an ache in the back of her throat. "It hurt so much to think I had lost you already when I had only just found you."

He gathered her in, so he had both of those big arms around her at last. He kissed her hair. "I'm here. I'm… stepping up."

She sighed and leaned her head on his broad chest. *Home,* she thought. *Right here. This is my home.* "This moment?" She made the two words a question.

"Yeah?"

"This is the best Christmas present I've ever received." Tears welled then. He must have heard them in her voice because he tipped her chin up again and bent close to kiss those tears away.

When he lifted his head, he whispered, "I'm ashamed to tell you…"

She held his gaze. "Anything. Whatever's bothering you, whatever needs saying, you can say it to me. You *have* to say it to me. You have to give us a chance to work through the things that are getting in our way."

"I'm afraid, that's all. I'm shaking in my boots. And a man doesn't like to admit he's afraid."

She searched his face. "But why?"

He sucked in a slow breath, as though drawing in courage right along with the oxygen. "Maybe your folks won't like me, won't approve of your hooking up with some small-town horse rancher."

"Oh, Preston…"

"Don't make light of that. Please." The words seemed dredged up from the deepest part of him. "It's not a light thing. Not to me. That you might turn to me one day and suddenly realize that I'm not smooth or sophisticated, that I'm not from your world. That you'll end up wondering what you ever saw in me."

She hastened to reassure him. "I wouldn't. I'm not. And in all the ways that matter, we *are* from the same world. You are stalwart and true-hearted. You are strong and good and you only want to do the right thing. You are all the things a man should be—all the things I've ever dreamed of in a man."

"You make me sound like some...shining ideal of manly perfection." There was humor in his eyes now.

And she was glad to see it. "That is exactly what you are—and as far as your being worried my family won't accept you, don't be. Wait until you meet them. They respect the things that really count in a person, things like honesty and keeping your word and living up to your agreements. And they want real happiness for their children. As long as I find the right man for me, they will be happy for me."

"Guess I'll have to take your word for it."

"Just wait. You'll see."

He caught her hand, brought it to his lips. "I know that it's only been three weeks since I first saw you, but I am certain of what's in my heart. These last few days of being apart from you, even though we've both been right here in the same house...these last few days have made me see the truth. It's too late for me to walk away and not get hurt. I...." He hesitated, drew in another slow breath. And then, at last, he said it. "I love you, Belle."

Pure happiness filled her. "Oh, Preston. I love you, too."

"I want us to be a family—you and me and Ben. And my dad and Charlotte. All together. I think we could make a good life, you and me."

"I do, too. Absolutely."

"I'm willing to talk about moving to Montedoro. I guess a man can raise horses there as well as here."

She shook her head. "I don't think that will be necessary. But I will need to travel. I have my work."

He didn't even hesitate. "Of course. As long as you come home to me."

"Always. Oh, yes."

"And sometimes, maybe, Ben and I could come along. I think it would be good for him. And for me. To get out, see the world, to see firsthand the work you do—and you don't have to say yes yet. You can…take your time. Think it over."

"Preston."

"What?"

"Are you listening?"

"You know that I am."

"Then I have thought it over and the answer is yes."

"Belle." He whispered her name like a sacred prayer. "You've been through a lot, losing Anne, coming all the way to Montana just to give up the little boy you only wanted to keep."

"Did you hear me, Preston? Yes."

"I'm going to ask you again next month. And the month after that. You need time. I'm not going to push you."

"What part of yes is unclear to you, Preston?"

"No part of yes is unclear to me. Just…humor me, won't you?"

She couldn't help but smile. "Yes. That is my answer. Now, next month—and always."

He kissed her. And then he said so tenderly, "Now, *that's* the best Christmas present *I* ever had."

Epilogue

Three months later

Captain Marcus Desmarais had been home for more than a month now.

He'd been proud to serve as security for Her Highness Arabella during her recent extended stay in the United States. He had great respect and admiration for the princess—for all of the Bravo-Calabretti family.

And when Her Highness had decided to marry the father of her lost friend's baby, Marcus had been offered the chance to make the assignment in Montana permanent. He had turned down the offer.

Marcus was Montedoran to the core. He was proud to go where his country needed him. But to leave Montedoro for years?

Never.

His life was here, in the country of his birth. He had

come from nothing, up through the Sovereign's Guard and into the newly formed Covert Command Unit created by His Highness Alexander, third-born of the four Bravo-Calabretti princes. Marcus loved his work and he was advancing swiftly and steadily. He lived to serve his country.

And his new orders should be up on the CCU website that day. Marcus fully expected another security assignment, which meant another trip out of the homeland most likely. Being a bodyguard to the princely family was an honor and he was good at it.

The CCU was a force of only fifty: fifty of Montedoro's best, brightest and strongest. Montedoro had no standing army. There was the Sovereign's Guard and the Civil Defense Corps. Beyond the Guard and the Corps, it was for the CCU to do it all, from providing protection for the princely family, to extracting Montedoran citizens from wrongful imprisonment worldwide, to targeting and eliminating threats to Montedoran security and the safety of its people.

At a little before nine that morning, Marcus entered his office cubicle at CCU headquarters not far from the Prince's Palace. He turned on his computer and logged in to the CCU site.

The orders were there, as expected.

One look at them had his stomach dropping into his boots and his blood spurting so furiously through his veins that he felt as though his head would explode. He had to read the cursed thing through several times before he finally accepted what he saw.

He was to provide personal security for Her Serene Highness Rhiannon, who would be attending her sister's wedding in Montana with the rest of the princely family.

Rhia. He thought the forbidden form of her name before he could stop himself. *This cannot be happening.*

He wouldn't *let* it happen. Surely there had to be some way to…

He cut the pointless notion short. He had his orders and there was no getting out of them. To try and change them would only draw attention to the fact that he wanted them changed. It would have the higher-ups asking questions he didn't want anyone to ask, lest they somehow stumble upon the answer.

There was nothing to do but accept the inevitable. He was a soldier. He would do his duty and do it well. The past was the past.

It was years ago. It never should have happened.

He would wipe it from his mind.

* * * * *

Watch for Rhiannon and Marcus's story,
HER HIGHNESS AND THE BODYGUARD,
coming in April 2013,
only from Harlequin Special Edition.

REQUEST YOUR FREE BOOKS!

2 FREE NOVELS PLUS 2 FREE GIFTS!

♦ Harlequin®

SPECIAL EDITION

Life, Love & Family

YES! Please send me 2 FREE Harlequin® Special Edition novels and my 2 FREE gifts (gifts are worth about $10). After receiving them, if I don't wish to receive any more books, I can return the shipping statement marked "cancel." If I don't cancel, I will receive 6 brand-new novels every month and be billed just $4.49 per book in the U.S. or $5.24 per book in Canada. That's a saving of at least 14% off the cover price! It's quite a bargain! Shipping and handling is just 50¢ per book in the U.S. and 75¢ per book in Canada.* I understand that accepting the 2 free books and gifts places me under no obligation to buy anything. I can always return a shipment and cancel at any time. Even if I never buy another book, the two free books and gifts are mine to keep forever.

235/335 HDN FEGF

Name	(PLEASE PRINT)

Address	Apt. #

City	State/Prov.	Zip/Postal Code

Signature (if under 18, a parent or guardian must sign)

Mail to the **Reader Service:**
IN U.S.A.: P.O. Box 1867, Buffalo, NY 14240-1867
IN CANADA: P.O. Box 609, Fort Erie, Ontario L2A 5X3

Not valid for current subscribers to Harlequin Special Edition books.

Want to try two free books from another line?
Call 1-800-873-8635 or visit www.ReaderService.com.

* Terms and prices subject to change without notice. Prices do not include applicable taxes. Sales tax applicable in N.Y. Canadian residents will be charged applicable taxes. Offer not valid in Quebec. This offer is limited to one order per household. All orders subject to credit approval. Credit or debit balances in a customer's account(s) may be offset by any other outstanding balance owed by or to the customer. Please allow 4 to 6 weeks for delivery. Offer available while quantities last.

Your Privacy—The Reader Service is committed to protecting your privacy. Our Privacy Policy is available online at www.ReaderService.com or upon request from the Reader Service.

We make a portion of our mailing list available to reputable third parties that offer products we believe may interest you. If you prefer that we not exchange your name with third parties, or if you wish to clarify or modify your communication preferences, please visit us at www.ReaderService.com/consumerchoice or write to us at Reader Service Preference Service, P.O. Box 9062, Buffalo, NY 14269. Include your complete name and address.

HSE11B

Turn the page for a preview of
THE OTHER SIDE OF US
by
Sarah Mayberry,
coming January 2013
from Harlequin® Superromance®.

PLUS, exciting changes are in the works!
Enjoy the same great stories in a longer format
and new look—beginning January 2013!

HSREXPINTRO2012

THE OTHER SIDE OF US
A brand-new novel
from Harlequin® Superromance® author
Sarah Mayberry

In recovery from a serious accident, Mackenzie Williams
is beating all the doctors' predictions. But she needs
single-minded focus. She doesn't *need the distraction*
of neighbors—especially good-looking ones
like Oliver Garrett!

MACKENZIE BREATHED DEEPLY to recover from the work-
out. She'd pushed herself too far but she wanted to accelerate
her rehabilitation. Still, she needed to lie down to combat
the nausea and shaking muscles.

There was a knock on the front door. Who on earth
would be visiting her on a Thursday morning? Probably a
cold-calling salesperson.

She answered, but her pithy rejection died before she'd
formed the first words.

The man on her doorstep was definitely not a cold caller.
Nothing about this man was cold, from the auburn of his
wavy hair to his brown eyes to his sensual mouth. Nothing
cold about those broad shoulders, flat belly and lean hips,
either.

"Hey," he said in a shiver-inducing baritone. "I'm Oliver
Garrett. I moved in next door." His smile was so warm and
vibrant it was almost offensive.

"Mackenzie Williams." Oh, no. Her legs were starting to

tremble, indicating they wouldn't hold up long. Any second now she would embarrass herself in front of this complete and very good-looking stranger.

"It's been years since I was down here." He seemed to settle in for a chat. "It doesn't look as though—"

"I have to go." Her stomach rolled as she shut the door. The last thing she registered was the look of shock on Oliver's face at her abrupt dismissal.

And somehow she knew their neighborly relations would be a lot cooler now.

Will Mackenzie be able to make it up to Oliver for her rude introduction? Find out in THE OTHER SIDE OF US by Sarah Mayberry, available January 2013 from Harlequin® Superromance®. PLUS, exciting changes are in the works! Enjoy the same great stories in a longer format and new look—beginning January 2013!